John's Love

A Love to Remember

A NOVEL BY
J. J. VALENTIN

This is a work of fiction. All the characters and events portrayed in this novel are fictitious.

John's Love

For the sheep

JOHN'S LOVE

1

CHAPTER ONE

One thousand years have passed in the Heavens, marking the beginning of the Trial period. For every one thousand years, two soul mates are chosen to be reborn in order to test their love and faith through the trials and tribulations of life's false reality. No soul is guaranteed to make it back or find each other; only through true love and tested faith will they then be reunited in the heavens as one again.

BELLS RING

TRUMPETS SOUND

SOUL MATES GATHER TOGETHER

A BLINDING LIGHT SHINES UPON JOHN AND SARAH as they stand amongst a crowd of countless souls. The time has come for them to fall back into life and forget all that they have experienced in the heavens.

John turns to Sarah, fighting back any signs of worry, grabs her hands and tries to comfort her with a smile. "I love you, sweetheart. Our love is unconditional and can never be forgotten. We shall rise out of love, through all."

Sarah begins to tear, barely able to reply, "God has made you for me, and me for you. We will—we'll forever be one."

Aware of the possibilities of never reuniting, they desperately cling to one another; Sarah shakes, but John holds firm.

With their hands held tightly together, they are thrown down toward the earth. Never once does their eyes disconnect as they fall through the earth's atmosphere and slowly fade away.

With one last breath, Sarah pleads, "Remember me! Remember me, Jo—"

*　　　*　　　*　　　*　　　*
　　*　　*　　　　*　*
*　　　*　　　*　　　*　　　*

"Hahaha!" Sarah laughs at her girlfriend's joke as they stand outside on the steps behind their high school.

At that very moment, John and his friends are walking across the basketball courts when he hears Sarah's loud, boisterous laugh. Somehow it seems familiar to him, so he looks to his left, and there she is with her long black hair, blowing in the wind, and her one-of-a-kind, genuine smile. His eyes and mind are locked on her as he is instantly reminded of whom she is and what she means to him: flashbacks of their past lives—in heaven and on Earth—flood his mind heavily. He tries to shake it off, thinking it might just be Déjà Vu, but he can't; he's stuck in this moment of love as if his life has just been pieced together. While his friends are talking, he hears nothing but her laugh, sees nothing but her smile, and is deeply in love with her goofy body movement as he watches her crack up in the distance. He doesn't know where these thoughts and feelings are coming from, but it's as if he's known her all along. From a single glance at a girl he's never met before, his soul cries desperately for love.

"*Sarah*," he gasps, nearly stopping in his tracks.

It is in this moment that John is transformed from an innocent teenage boy to a man enlightened by love; it is in this moment that destiny strikes, and John's trials and tribulations begin.

*　　　*　　　*　　　*　　　*
　　*　　*　　　　*　　*
*　　　*　　　*　　　*　　　*

The Angels in heaven watch down on John, confused by how he remembers his past life; it's not supposed to happen, nor has it ever happened before. The rebirth of soul mates is supposed to be routine: fate is supposed to blindly pull them together as long as they remain good beings and stay faithful to God. Yet, somehow, fate is no longer in charge of their destiny; it has taken a turn and put itself into John's hands. And the Angels know that the consequences of this knowledge can be drastic: if he makes the wrong choices, he can alter their future and past all at once. He and Sarah need to fall in love in order to secure their destiny—but more importantly, Layla, their destined daughter, needs them to become one in order to even exist, or else she will fade like a sunset that never rises again.

Panic begins to stir in the heavens, knowing John's visions will inevitably become more of a burden than a blessing during these modern times on Earth. The Angels know that Satan will twist and manipulate John by using his visions against him, through the human mentality and notion that what is in front of you is all that exist—that what you can *see* and *feel* is the true and *only* reality. So they make plans to help influence John and Sarah's love in order to combat the evil that will try to overshadow their destiny, until they hear God's voice thunder in the heavenly skies:

"YOU WILL DO NOTHING TO HELP THESE SOULS. LET LOVE AND FAITH GUIDE THE WAY, AND PRAY THEY TAKE THAT ROAD. IT IS THEIR DESTINY TO WRITE, NOT YOURS. WHEN IT IS TIME, I WILL BE THERE."

As the day fades and the night rolls in, John paces back and forth in his room, trying to make sense of his irrational thoughts. The visions, and immense passion that came with them, have now grown into a dark, disabling paranoia; he has become consumed with the disturbing fear of possibly losing his mind.

Knowing schizophrenia has burdened many of his family, John sweats through every pore as the panic within quickly takes over. The anxiety soon becomes too much, and he desperately seeks for answers by searching the internet into the wee hours of the morning. He reads every possible article and forum on schizophrenia that he can, and only confirms his fears the more he reads on: delusions, hallucinations... inability to determine reality. Suddenly, it all makes sense. He's always felt out of place in life and now he's found the reason.

. . . .

After hours of obsessing over his mental health, he exhausts himself but still isn't able—or willing—to rest. The nerve-racking thought of being ill weighs too heavily on his mind to even attempt to sleep, so he decides to try to clear his head by sitting on the floor in a meditative state. Taking a deep breath, he sits on the floor with his back against the wall and puts his knees up to his chest. He drops his head to his knees, closes his eyes and rocks back and forth to try to sooth the panic that's waiting to erupt.

THE FRESHEST OF ALL AIR AND RICHEST of all scents begins to fill John's lungs. With his eyes shut and head down, he hears distant waters flowing and animals of all kinds around him.

He lifts his head and realizes he is no longer sitting with his back against his wall, but in the middle of what seems to be a forest; and yet, somehow, he feels warm and comforted with a calm. He is not scared of all that he sees or all that he hears, only filled with one of man's greatest gifts: curiosity.

He gets up, wipes his clothes and looks up toward the treetops and bright, clear blue sky and is fascinated by the scenery as different flocks of birds fly above while lions, zebras and water buffalo walk peacefully past him. There are no longer any predators or prey where he is; all that exists coexist.

Filled with excitement, he makes his way toward the sounds of the waters. As he gets closer to the sounds of what seems to be waterfalls or rivers, he can see people playing and laughing from afar.

"Hey!" he shouts, anxious to figure out where he is, and walks toward them, steadily picking up pace and waving his hands. But the closer he gets, the harder it is to lift his feet; it's as if gravity increases to keep him away.

Suddenly, his feet become stuck to the ground.

The blue skies then begin to grey, and the pleasant sounds of animals coexisting gradually turn into screams from prey. All of the trees are no longer green and blowing in the wind, but dead and still. The fresh air becomes smothered with a distinct scent of burnt wood and dead animal corpses. And the calm that once eased John has gone, leaving him to tremble in fear.

Though it's only been mere minutes, John feels like he's spent an eternity in sorrow as a deep depression falls over him. His only glimmer of hope comes from the sight of those that are playing and laughing in the distance as his soul fights the darkness by reminding him of whom they are. Infinite times rush through his mind revealing their truth: they are his family, all which have come before and after him.

"Help," he pleads, with a faint voice, stretching out his hand toward them, but gets no response.

"Help ... help me. Help!" he screams out. "Somebody! *Anybody* ... help."

His cry for help falls on deaf ears.

After several minutes of staring desperately into the distance, even his glimmer of hope fades, as they too fade away in an envelope of darkness.

There's no longer anyone or anything around him; he can only hear the horror screams of tortured prey, and soon even they go silent. He's left in a dark abyss with nothing but the sound of his own fear as he begins to hyperventilate.

"What's happening!" he screams out again. "Someone help!!"

A woman sobs within the darkness. "I'm sorry. I'm so, so sorry." Then a voice of a young girl cries out, "Daddy, I'm scared."

John quickly covers his ears, but their cries come from within; he's hopeless in stopping their torment.

The young girl's cries heighten, "Daddy, please!! Don't let Mommy go!"

The truth behind her cries begins to shed light on where he is as John is filled with vivid memories of Sarah and Layla. He falls to his knees and tears rush down his face from an overwhelming fear that he may never see them again, or if they're even real.

The anxiety of possibly being crazy begins to consume his mind and causes him to shake uncontrollably. *This can't be real*, he tells himself, hoping it's all a dream and trying to wake from it.

The young girl's torment only intensifies the more he tries to ignore it, and his arms fall hopelessly to his sides knowing there's nothing he can do to stop it. His hands are then forced behind his back and cuffed, and his head begins to pound as if he was just hit head-on by a freight truck. Then, suddenly, he begins to age.

"What's happening?" he utters in pain as blood trickles down his face, creating a puddle around him.

Satan within the darkness responds, "You will never see these people again because they do not exist. All that you think you see, or seen, is nothing more than a figment of your imagination. Nothing is, or was, ever real. Except this moment, this cold, empty, sorrowful moment that has *all* been caused by you. This is your reality. Life is not a blessing. It is torture. And love does not exist. Tell me, do you feel love *now*?"

John's skin crawls from the sound of Satan's voice.

"This darkness. This hole. This inescapable emptiness that you feel is all that ever was and all that ever will be. Even I am just an illusion—a projection of your truest thoughts."

Walking out of the darkness, Satan finally reveals himself, and John's eyes widen from the sight of a man of his own image. But although the man before his eyes is of him, John knows he is only a dark manifestation that embodies pure hate and evil; a man of great tragedy and sorrow lies behind the red eyes of this false version of him.

Satan throws his hands up, saying, "I am you. I am reality. I am your mind. The genetic disease that has burdened your family is starting to spark in you. You're schizophrenic, but you can stop it. Unlike them, you have the power to overcome these delusions. Don't seek them. If you do, you will live a lie, and you will suffer in the end. And in the end, you'll end up just where you've started. Right here. Right now. Don't allow your foolish thoughts to become you, John. You're stronger than that. Look at me." Satan points to himself. "I am the outcome of all the pain and suffering you will endure if you do not leave behind these delusions that you call 'love' and wake up to reality. Wake up! Wake up, John! Wake—"

"Wake up, John. Wake up," says Gail, John's mother, nudging him gently.

He's lying on his stomach with his face pressed against the cold hardwood floor in his room.

"Hello? Why are you sleeping on the floor, John?"

He opens his eyes slowly, still traumatized by his dream, and remains silent.

"Are you okay, honey?"

He sits up and leans against the wall from where he fell asleep, scratching his head and nearly pinching himself to figure out if he's awake or still dreaming.

"John, I'm talking to you. Why are you sleeping on the floor?"

He takes a deep breath, exhales and tells her a lie to keep her from worrying: "I don't know. I must have fell off the bed or something. I don't—I don't remember."

"Well, get up and get ready for school. You're going to have to make yourself some breakfast today. I'm running late for work. Call me later when you get home, okay?"

He nods.

After she leaves his room and shuts his door, he rubs his face, wipes the crust from his eyes and leans his head back on the wall to try to collect himself. *It was just a dream. Oh, God, let it be just a dream.*

A shimmering light draws his eyes to the left and brings his attention to the gold lettering on the spine of his Bible that is sitting on his bookcase. It's as if it were saying, "Open me."

In secret, John has always been a religious kid. He'd always read his Bible regularly, especially in times of great agony. This is one of those times.

Even though he's been awake for several minutes, he still questions his reality. He's tormented by the idea that his life—or life in general—is just one big delusion, as foretold in his dream.

Taking a deep breath, he stands on his two feet, walks toward his bookcase, grabs his Bible and whispers with his eyes closed in prayer: "Give me a sign, Lord, that this life is real and all of that was just a nightmare. Show me the reason for these thoughts that I have. Help me understand. Help me *believe*."

Gail opens his door.

He panics and throws his Bible across the room, onto his bed. His heart beats rapidly, hoping she didn't see him or else he would have to think of a quick lie. He doesn't want her to worry about him, or his mental state; she's already been through enough with her brother suffering from schizophrenia, as is.

"John, I'm leaving, honey. I left your lunch money on the table."

He exhales in relief, knowing she's seen nothing. "Thanks, Mom. I'll see you later, love you."

"Love you too, hun." She blows him a kiss and then closes his door, and he immediately runs over to his bed and picks up his Bible, which is facedown and open to The Gospel of John.

He's thrown back by the title because it bears his name, but it's not enough of a sign.

Coincidence, he tells himself, skimming through each passage, hoping to find something more concrete. He finally lands on John 3:3:

"Very truly I tell you, no one can see the kingdom of God without being born again."

2

CHAPTER TWO

The school doors open and students roam through the halls to get to their morning classes. John is within the crowd, keeping his head up to find Sarah.

He turns the corner, and there she is, with her back turned away from him, quietly unloading her books for the day. The world seems to slow down and blur as his eyes can only focus in on her. His mind then begins to race, thinking of ways to introduce himself:

Hi, love.—No.
Do you know who I am?—No.
Hi, Sarah, I'm John.—Okay.

He finally finds the courage and makes his way over to her, but Tommy Devoe, the school player, beats him to it. John can't stand the sight of him—let alone watch him talk to Sarah—but he's forced to stop at a distance and wait for his moment. His eyes and ears are locked into their conversation as he waits impatiently in the distance. And every time Sarah smiles, blushes and twirls her hair, John's confidence dies.

Feeling as if someone is watching her, Sarah looks back, but no one is there. John has left.

She shrugs it off, looks back at Tommy, smiles and continues to converse.

. . . .

At 12:15 the lunch bell rings. Everyone goes to the same place for lunch every day, Rey's. Sarah typically stays in school and enjoys lunch alone in the library. But today, she agreed to go get a bite with Tommy. And while John and his friends are normally the first to arrive at Rey's, they're running late because of a basketball meeting.

Anxious to get out and see if Sarah and Tommy are at Rey's like everyone else, John fidgets in his seat and bites at his nails. The clock seems to tick slower every time he stares at its hands, and his coach doesn't seem to care much for his team's time to eat, either.

After a lengthy meeting, that nearly killed the team's lunchtime, the boys are let out. And although John's first instinct is to run to the pizzeria to ensure Sarah will still be there, he can't leave his teammates behind. They go everywhere as a pack, so he must swallow his urges and calmly walk with them to avoid any suspicious behavior.

When they arrive at Rey's, the atmosphere is filled with student laughter, bets and healthy arguments debating strategies to defeat rival schools in upcoming games. John's greeted by friends, and he embraces each one while looking through his peripheral to see if Sarah is there. He spots her sitting quietly in the corner next to Tommy, not saying much, just agreeing to most of what he is telling or asking her.

Hearing John's voice, Sarah's attention quickly drifts from Tommy and onto him, and she smiles to herself. She's always been the quiet girl in the corner of the room while the lights shined bright on John, always been the girl who loved him from a distance but never dared to say hello. Her intentions to go to lunch with Tommy were solely to be closer to John, to possibly muster up the courage to finally say hi.

"Hey, John, over here!" yells Adam, one of his team-mates, who's pointing at an open seat next to him, which just happens to be right across from Sarah.

"Hold on, let me grab a bite!" John shouts back. He orders two slices and a coke and then makes his way over to the table.

"John, this is Tommy and...I'm sorry, I'm drawing a blank. What's your name again?"

"Sarah," John answers. "Her name is Sarah."

She smiles from ear to ear, captured by John's eyes. There's something about the way he looks at her that feels like home. "Yes, that's right. Sarah Lewis. How'd you know?"

John shrugs his shoulders, smiles and tells a lie: "I guessed." He then extends his hand to her, unable to think of anything else to say. He's thought of so many ways to say hello throughout the day yet is nearly speechless when she's brought to him. And a girl with an endless vocabulary and an IQ higher than most is also at a loss for words. She's seen him a thousand times over the years but has never been able to look into his eyes as she is now.

"Hi, John, it's nice to meet—"

"You're beautiful," he lets out, unable to hold it in any longer.

She blushes hearing words not many have spoken to her yet the boy of her dreams has just uttered them.

Tommy turns red, furious at the disrespect John has shown him. But John has no respect for the person Tommy is, so he has no need to be friendly.

Tommy clinches his hands, ready for a fight. "What do you think you're doing? You think you can talk to my girl like that?"

Sarah jerks her head at Tommy. "Excuse me? I'm not your girl. Please stop."

Everyone becomes silent, noticing the confrontation. They wait anxiously for what John is going to say.

John's blood boils as he stares Tommy down. But instead of fighting, he takes a different approach. He smirks at Tommy and asks, "Who are you?"

"What?"

"Who are you?" he asks again.

"Who am I?" Tommy laughs, showboats his physique and looks around the room at everyone and then back at John. "Are you serious? Everyone here knows me. Don't play stupid."

John nods his head and chuckles beneath his breath. "I don't think you understand. I know your name. I even know your reputation. But who are you?"

The confusion on Tommy's face humors John as he continues to play his psychological game.

"What the hell are you talking about?"

Poised and calm, John continues, "Who are you, really? I mean, I see your snapback and name-brand clothing, but who are you? Who is Tommy? Because all I see is a phony, a wannabe—a copycat. What you are others have been years before your time. You're nothing new, just a worthless womanizer with no originality. Muscle without a brain. A peacock flapping its wings. Now let me ask you, how high can a peacock fly?"

John's words cut deep, and Tommy is left without an answer, so he does exactly what John thought he would: he kicks his own seat from under him and stands over John, broadening his shoulders and playing right into his game.

Within seconds, John's teammates surround Tommy. He's in John's world now and learns that quickly. His large stature is no match for the loyalty of good friends.

"Is everything all right, John?" asks Caesar, owner of Rey's and good friend of John's family.

"Everything's fine. I was actually just about to leave." John looks over at Sarah. "Would you like to come with me?"

All eyes lie on her as she tries her best to hold back the redness in her cheeks.

She grins and agrees to leave with a simple nod, and John doesn't waste a moment. He extends his hand and she grabs on without a second thought, and they leave Rey's the same way they left heaven, together, hand in hand.

3
CHAPTER THREE

John and Sarah have gone on vacation together as a high-school graduation present from both of their parents, knowing they won't be able to see each other as much as they'd like since John will be leaving for New York in the fall to study architecture while Sarah remains in New Jersey to study nursing.

LYING ON THE BEACH OF THE CALIFORNIA SHORE, with sand between their toes and their bodies warmed in each other's arms, they gaze up at the abundance of stars in the clear night sky and allow their minds to drift off in thought as they listen to the sounds of the crashing waves.

"Do you believe in life after death, John? Heaven and Hell?"

He doesn't say a word for a moment, just gazes into her eyes, wishing she could read between his and not force him to lie, because he knows if he tells her about his visions she'd think he was mad. So he covers up his answers with *maybes* and *what-ifs*. "I do. What if this life is just a test to achieve a greater life beyond our imagination, and death was nothing more than a doorway to the beginning?"

"A test?"

"Yes, a test. A test of love."

"What do you mean?"

"What if life was all about love? What if we were the manifestation of a great creator's love—the embodiment of the pure and unconditional love of God—and all we have to do in this life is produce more of it?"

"More of what?" Sarah asks, truly lost.

"Love."

"How do you create love?"

"Children. Daughters, sons, grandchildren and so on," he answers, hoping something will click.

She blushes thinking he has an ulterior motive. "Are you trying to get in my pants, John?"

He chuckles realizing his story of destiny isn't coming out the way he intended. "No, I'm not. Although . . . " he jokes back. "But what if I told you that up there, in the sky, where the stars shine brightest, was our daughter looking down on us?"

Sarah looks at him with a smirk on her face, still believing he's only trying to sleep with her, and then playfully pulls on his shirt and places her lips inches from his, ready to give him what she thinks he really wants.

He moves her hair from her face, seeing Layla in her beautiful green eyes, and continues to explain: "What if love was always, and has always been, destined? What if everyone that has ever existed, and will ever exist, already exists in this very moment? What if those that are living now, like you and I, have their entire destined family looking down on their lives like a film being played in a theatre? Sons and daughters watch their parents' love story unfold right before their very eyes as they wait for the day of their birth."

Sarah thinks of the possibility and falls in love with it, but of course, she's skeptical. She's always been a realist and views the world as a glass half empty rather than full.

"Well, wouldn't that be the most amazing book, ever!" she jokes. "But I don't know, John. I love the idea. I really do. I think it's beautiful. But wouldn't that mean that life was all planned out? That everyone is a slave to their own destiny and nothing can be changed? What would be the point of life if everyone went by a plan? And what about the lives of those who suffer every day due to their health, their finances or simply trying to find something to eat? Is that their destiny? Doesn't that seem cruel to you? Sure, a love story is always beautiful to think about, but this life has a lot more bad than good in it. It *can't* be destined."

John looks at her in an endearing way, knowing she'll always have a rebuttal for anything fantastic. "That's the thing. Maybe our lives *are* written, but maybe, *just maybe*, we also have our own choices. And with those choices, we either follow our storylines or drift off to create new ones—for better or worse."

Sarah squints, not buying into it.

"Look, I'm not saying everyone's story is going to be great or even have a 'happy' ending, but I do think that everyone has a purpose. Maybe we just aren't meant to know what that purpose is right now. Maybe all we can do is just live the lives we're given and wait to be graded as if it were a test from God."

"Well, what if our stories were to change? How would that work out for our children?" she questions, finding another hole in John's theory.

"What do you mean?"

"You said that up there, where the stars shine brightest, is where our daughter looks down on us. So I'm asking, what would happen if we made the wrong choices, or what if two soul mates, like you and I"—she caresses his face—"never fall in love or even meet? What would happen to the 'destined' children, then?"

John's stumped. He never thought about that possibility. Suddenly his visions don't make sense.

Sarah quickly realizes, through his silence, that she's thrown out a question he can't answer. And although she does not believe in his theory, she also doesn't want to kill his dream, so she continues to entertain the idea. "What would be her name?" she asks, but gets no response. John's mind is deep in thought, trying to make sense of his visions of Layla as he desperately looks up toward the stars.

"What would be her name?" she asks again, poking him to bring his attention back to her.

"Huh? Whose name?"

"Our daughter. What would be her name?"

"I don't—I don't know," he answers, troubled by her rebuttal. "Why don't you ask her yourself?" He points to the sky. "Maybe she'll tell you."

Sarah becomes quiet and thinks of many names like a child playing house.

"Um, Layla. I like that name. *Layla* it's a pretty name, isn't it?"

John leans his forehead against hers, looks deep into her eyes and tells her a truth within a sweet whisper: "*Layla* it is."

She smiles and her eyes glisten, knowing that he would truly love to build a family with her. "What if we had a son? A boy that looks just like you."

"I don't think we will."

"Come on, I picked out our girl's name. Now it's your turn to pick out our boy's. It's only right."

John shrugs his shoulders and says nothing.

"Ugh, fine. I'll choose one myself. How about Jake? I've always liked that name. What do you think?"

"Eh, Layla is *much* better," John cracks.

Sarah smirks. "Men and their girls."

He brings Sarah closer into his arms and holds her tight as she looks up at the twinkling sky and allows her mind to dream.

"Will you love me forever, John?" she asks playfully, yet waiting for the perfect answer.

And with three words, he delivers the truth, "Longer than that."

4
CHAPTER FOUR

In the evening of a school night, Sarah sits at her desk in her dorm room with her hair in a bun, a cup of coffee in one hand, a pen in the other, and her eyes pierced to her laptop's screen as she prepares for an all-nighter. She's a strong, independent woman who's very much motivated and focused on her career and life goals, especially now that John is far away. Her achievements are not only for her own success but are seen as stepping-stones to the ultimate goal: a life no longer separated from John. Day in and day out, she works with him on her mind, as he does the same for her. But everyone, even Sarah, has their bad influences.

JENN AND CASEY, SARAH'S ROOMATES, WALK IN and sit around her as her eyes are glued to her laptop's screen. Jenn sits on her own bed while Casey sits with her legs criss-crossed on the floor; both stare at Sarah like two children waiting to ask a question.

"What do you want?" Sarah grunts, still keeping her eyes pierced to the screen; she knows they're up to something.

"Come on, Sarah, it's Wednesday. You know what that means?" Jenn asks.

"Ladies Night!" Casey shouts.

"Yes!" Jenn shouts back, holding a bottle of vodka in one hand and cranberry juice in the other as she bounces up and down her bed. "Would you please, please, *please* come out with us for once? I'll beg. Do you want me to beg?"

"No thanks."

"Come on, you're always studying. We never get to hang out! You could be a doctor, or whatever it is that you want to be, tomorrow. But tonight is Ladies Night!"

"Hey! That's not fair. I go out with you guys all the time. In the weekend. Like normal people."

"Well, normal people, *whoever they are*"—Jenn sarcastically throws up her hands—"are boring."

Casey rolls her eyes in agreement. "Yeah! And when you do come out, it's always with John."

Sarah stops typing and turns around. "So what? That's my boyfriend. He was my boyfriend before I even met you guys. What's wrong with me hanging out with him? I only get to see him in the weekend, for not *nearly* enough time, and yet I still make time for you both, even while he's here."

"That's. Our. Point," Casey argues back.

"And what's that?"

"We don't want to hang out with you *and* John. We want to hang out with *you*."

"Exactly," Jenn puts in her two cents. "All you ever talk about is John. John this. John that. John, John, John. You've never even really had the chance to live your life. You've both been together since you were kids. Don't you want to experience new things? Everything is either about him or with him. Don't get us wrong, we think he's a great guy—even though we're sure he hates us—and you two are perfect for each other, but we want you to enjoy your college life. *These are the years, Sarah.* You can't get them back. It's been a year already, three semesters, and you barely stepped out of this room."

Sarah's face says it all. "What do you mean John doesn't like you? Of course he does. What about the times—and there were many—when he paid for everyone's dinner and treated us all to a movie? I don't remember you saying anything then. But now that I don't feel like going out, he's to blame? Look, I'm sorry that you feel like I don't spend enough time with you guys, but I'm extremely busy juggling school and a relationship—long distance, at that. And it's a *real* relationship, not like you'd both understand, anyway. Neither of you have had a relationship longer than, what, a month? You two are so busy sleeping with Tom, Dick and Harry every other weekend that you wouldn't know a good guy if he was standing right in front of you waving flowers and screaming your name." Sarah takes a moment and looks at them as they hold their heads down like two punished children. "Ugh, *fine*... I'll go out with you guys tonight."

"Yeess!" Jenn and Casey scream. "The trio is back!!"

. . . .

For most of the night, the girls spend their time singing karaoke and taking shots innocently together until Jenn and Casey decide to talk to two guys across the room and leave Sarah alone at the bar, sipping on a Long Island.

Bored and over the bar scene, Sarah reaches into her purse for her phone to text John, only to discover it isn't there.

"Damn it," she mutters.

"Can I help you?" asks a gentleman as he pulls a seat up next to her and sits down.

"No," she responds, dismissing him, not giving him the time of day or even turning around to acknowledge him.

"Okay. I'm just trying to help, that's all. I'll leave you alone. I get it."

"Ugh, I'm sorry. I'm not trying to be rude or anything. Tonight just isn't going very well for—" she turns around to speak face to face and is stunned by how handsome he is. He's got a glow to him that can't be explained but certainly his slick black hair, expensive suit and the sweet smell of his cologne helps "—um, I . . . I lost my phone. There isn't anything you can do to help. But thank you, anyway. I'm sorry for being rude. I'm sure you're a nice guy."

"Here, use mine to call yours. It has to be around here somewhere."

"Oh, thanks! I didn't even think about that. That's really nice of you." She takes his phone and searches all over the bar, hoping to see it light up or miraculously hear her ringtone through the loud music, but after a thorough search, it's nowhere to be found.

"It's gone. I can't find it." She forces a smile on her face and hands him back his phone. "Thank you for your help, though. That was really sweet of you."

"My pleasure, anytime. Can I buy you a drink?"

"No, thanks. I should be going now. I have to bring my friends home. Have a good night."

As she walks past him, he grabs her wrist and gently rubs his thumb across her soft skin, making her weak in the knees and stopping her in her tracks. "I never got your name."

She turns back around and slowly removes her wrist from his grasp. "It's Sarah. Have a good night, sir."

"You do the same," he responds, possessing her with his eyes and drawing out her lust.

She quickly heads over to her friends.

"Uh-oh, someone was having a good time over there," Jenn taunts.

"She sure was," Casey joins in.

"Don't worry, we won't tell John. Wait, who's John again?" Jenn laughs, fluttering her eyes at Sarah.

"Ha... ha... ha... very funny, guys. Come on, let's go." Sarah stretches out her hands and pulls her friends off of the laps of the two men.

The girls pout and walk off with Sarah.

"Look, Sarah, we won't tell anyone, but did you get that guys number? I know you did, didn't you?" Jenn playfully bumps Sarah.

Sarah rolls her eyes, feeling flustered and embarrassed. "I. Have. A. Boyfriend. What don't you understand?

"Let's be real, Sarah. You're only 19 years old and that is one *fine-ass* man over there. You never know, maybe he can teach you some things that John can't—" Casey giggles and winks her eye "—if you know what I mean."

Sarah looks back at Casey in disgust. "No. I didn't get anyone's number. He just lent me his phone so I can call mine. That's all. Nothing more. He didn't even ask me for mine, if you must know. He was just being nice."

"Yeah—" Jenn chuckles "—*right*. Like there's any guy in this world that's nice just to be *nice*. Get real, girl! You know men want one thing, and *one thing* only." Jenn and Casey slap Sarah's bottom.

"Ow! You girls are drunk. It's time to go. Give me your phone, so I can call a cab."

Jenn grunts and hands Sarah her cell. "Ugh, you're such a party-pooper."

. . . .

Jenn and Casey laugh obnoxiously loud as they drunkenly stumble into their dorm room.

"Shhh, be quiet. People are going to hear you," Sarah warns, quietly shutting her door.

They throw themselves on Sarah's bed and playfully cuddle with each other.

"Go to sleep. I can't even deal with you guys right now. You're both a mess."

Jenn and Casey giggle and continue to fix themselves into each other's arms until they doze off.

When the room is finally quiet, Sarah hears the fans spinning in her laptop.

She walks over to shut it down, and her eyes widen in excitement. "Yes!!" she shouts, thrilled to see her phone right next to it. "Thank you, God. Thank you, God. Thank. You. God!" She kisses and hugs it tight. "I must've forgotten you while we were pregaming."

"Shhh! Be quiet! People are going to *hear* you. We can't even deal with you right now!" the girls simultaneously shout, laughing hysterically at their own humor, and then quickly fall back into their drunken comas.

Sarah pays no mind to them as she scrolls through her phone. She has nine missed calls and one text: eight calls from a private number, one call and a text from John.

John's text reads:

Hey, babe. I just got out of work. Sorry I missed your call. I tried to call you back but you're probably asleep by now. Anyway, I'll talk to you tomorrow. Love you."

1:35 AM

She texts back:

Baby! I was actually out with the girls. I wish I stood home, though. I practically had to carry them home again. I know you're sleeping now, so I hope you're dreaming of me! lol<3"

4:00 AM

36

John's phone vibrates and wakes him from his sleep. He smiles at her text and texts back:

"Always do. Goodnight."

4:01 AM

then falls back asleep.

John's standing in the middle of a desolate street. The sun is set but no stars are out, and there are no lights on in any home. The only lights that shine are the street poles, and even they flicker on and off.

"Babe, where are you?" Sarah playfully shouts from a distance.

"I have no idea. Where are you?"

"Come find me!" she giggles, as if she's playing a game of hide-and-seek.

"Okay, can I get a clue?" he asks, trying to follow the sound of her voice.

"Over here!" A light turns on in the second story of a home, giving him a clear sign of where she is, and he runs over to the house.

When he arrives at the front door, it creaks itself open. The entire house is pitch-black except for a light shining through the edges of a closed door upstairs.

"Sarah?"

"There you go," she seductively whispers. "Come to me."

He walks up the stairs, and the closer he gets to the top, the heavier her moans become. Aroused and excited, he throws open the door...only to find Sarah in bed with another man.

She eerily smiles at him as the other man thrust himself into her, and points and laughs.

Frozen in place, John can't comprehend what he's seeing. His best friend, love, *soul mate* has just betrayed him in the worst way. And she mocks and emasculates him with the beauty that he first fell in love with. That beautiful, innocent, genuine laugh he once loved so much has now become an awful, torturous sound.

John tries to run at the man, but his feet instantly become stuck to the ground.

"She's mine," a demonic voice echoes into his ear, and John shakes with all the rage in the world. "Aahh—"

"—Aaahh!!" John screams, waking himself, breathing heavily and sweating profusely in his bed.

He sits himself up, wipes the sweat from his face and continues to take deep breaths. It's just a dream, *just a dream*, he tells himself, sickened to his stomach.

Throughout the day, he tries to shake off his nightmare, but is unable to. No matter how hard he tries, he can't help but fall victim to his own paranoia. His mind soon gets the best of him, and he decides to visit Sarah, needing to hold her to put his mind at ease.

Jenn hears a constant knock at the door and opens it. "Hey, John, what are you doing here?" she asks, flirtatiously biting her lip and toying with the buttons on her blouse. She's always had a thing for him. She's attracted to his good looks, but most of all the fact that he's a challenge because he's taken—even if it is by her best friend. There's no line she won't cross.

He nods, barely paying her any attention, and nearly walks through her to get to Sarah.

"Babe!" Sarah shouts, running out from the bathroom and jumping into his arms.

He passionately kisses her as if he hadn't seen her in years, and Jenn and Casey look on with jealousy in their eyes.

"What are you doing here?" she asks, grinning from ear to ear.

"I had to see you. I just, I needed to see you."

She blushes, looks at her friends and gestures her head to the door. They get the hint and walk out.

"Make sure you lock it!" Sarah shouts, laughing and giggling as she squeezes him tight.

He throws her on the bed, kisses her neck, and then runs his hand down her thigh as she runs hers through his hair. She tries to lift his shirt over his head, but it gets stuck. She pulls and pulls, but it won't give, and they laugh until it finally comes off.

She caresses his face and he kisses her palms, loving her touch. "There you go," she whispers, gazing into his eyes.

John's eyes widen in fear as he remembers those exact words in his dream. His heart begins to race, and he quickly looks away to hide his torment.

"What's wrong?" she asks.

He doesn't say a word.

"Come back to me," she whispers, as she continues to caress the stubbles on his face, slowly bringing his eyes back to her. "Where did you go?"

Again, he doesn't answer, but he pushes through his fear and begins to make love to her. And she breathes heavily, excited by his passion.

But just as things begin to heat up, her phone rings repeatedly.

"Leave it," she tells him, forcing his head to her breasts.

But the phone rings again, and John can sense the urgency of the caller.

"Here, just answer it," he says, reaching over to grab her phone from the nightstand. And as he hands it over to her, a text appears:

"Hey, babe, it was great meeting you last night. Hopefully you got your phone back and maybe, just maybe, you'll give me a call? :)"

6:35 PM

John looks at Sarah suspiciously. "Who's calling you 'babe' from this 212 number?"

"What?" She grabs her phone to read the text. "Uh, I don't know. Maybe they texted the wrong number."

"Who is this, Sarah?"

"I told you. I don't—Oh wait, I think I know who it might be."

"Who's that?"

"I don't know for sure, but it's probably this guy who lent me his phone last night."

"For what?"

"Let me finish. I thought I lost my cell around the bar, so he was nice enough to lend me his to call mine. He must've saved my number."

John knows he can trust Sarah, but he's still trying to get over his dream, so he's a bit apprehensive. "You didn't tell him you have a boyfriend?"

"John, really? Look, he sat at the bar next to me and asked if I needed anything. I told him I lost my phone, he lent me his and then I was on my way out the door. The conversation didn't last long enough to even tell him that I have—" she pauses for a moment, adoring his jealousy "— the *best* boyfriend in the world!" She smiles from ear to ear, hoping to relieve whatever is on his mind. She's surprised to see him jealous, she's never known him to be.

John fakes a smile, but she can see past it.

"Hey, you can trust me. You know you're my everything, right?"

"I know. I'm just afraid of losing you, that's all."

"You had my heart at sixteen, John, and you'll have it forever. You're *never* going to lose me, not even if you tried."

Comforted by her words, he pushes through his own torturous thoughts and makes love to her.

*   *   *   *   *
    *   *   *   *
*   *   *   *   *

The Angels in heaven celebrate as John manages to pull himself out of Satan's trickery and continue down the right path. Yet, while the heavens are filled with cheers of joy, Layla stands in silence.

"It's not over," she whispers to herself, sensing there is much more in store for her father.

5
CHAPTER FIVE

Months have passed, and just as the time has changed, so has John and Sarah's relationship. Even though they love each other just as much as ever, their school and work schedules have made it nearly impossible to see each other. The weekends they once shared have taken a backseat to John's long overnight shifts and Sarah's early-morning schedule, leaving them with only monthly visits. And while Sarah has tried many times to reschedule her shifts—and even looked for other jobs—John's ambition for "success" has overshadowed her cries for his love, causing tension between the two.

Sarah's phone rings. She picks up but doesn't say a word.

"Sarah, talk to me," John pleads. "We can't argue like this anymore. It's been two weeks since we've spoke. And every time I call, you answer but don't say a word. I know you're upset, but what is it that you want me to do? I *have* to work. It's a sacrifice. It's—"

"You're right," she lets out, with tears rimming her eyes. "There's nothing that you or I can do anymore. This is the end, John. We've tried."

John's end of the phone is silent. There's nothing worse that he could've ever heard.

"What do you mean?"

"I can't do this anymore. It's too hard."

"We can figure this out, Sarah. We've done it for this long. I just need a little more time, just a little while longer. I promise you, when it's all over you'll see more of me than you'd wish. I'll be with you day in and day out. But you have to give us a little more time."

Her voice breaks, "There's nothing to figure out. This won't work. I'm here and you're there. We've tried for months, and I can see us growing apart. You can deny it or see the tru—"

"I know the truth. It's you and I. It's always been you and me."

"Not anymore. I can't be the girl waiting on a dream that might never come true. Once upon a time, John, *once upon a time*, that's how it felt for us. It felt magical, but not anymore. We were great together. I'd rather look back and see it that way than to keep heading down this path. I can't fight anymore. I don't have it in me, I just don't. If it's meant to be, it'll—"

"I'm in a city!" John shouts. "I'm in a city where I know no one. I'm all by myself. No friends. No family. Nobody. So don't tell me what hard is. This is what it takes, Sarah. I can easily give up and come back home but then where would we be? How would we live? I'm not only doing this for me. You have to understand that I'm doing this for us. For our family. For our security. I know, *believe me*, I know you're lonely. It's all that I think about every night. But I'm begging you, *please*, you have to see the bigger picture."

Even though he delivers the right words, Sarah still feels the right thing to do is to let him go; she doesn't have hope like he does. He's always been a dreamer while she's been a realist; it's what made them so strong together. But today, her realistic mentality has torn them apart. The inability to imagine a better future beyond today's reality has overwhelmed her thoughts, her feelings, her love and her faith.

"The bigger picture doesn't have me and you in it," she coldly responds, hanging up on him, hoping that her disrespect will anger him so much that he gives up on her.

She throws her phone against the wall, breaking it into pieces, and bawls her eyes out.

John calls Sarah over and over again, but of course, he gets no answer. After several failed attempts, he puts on his coat, jumps on his motorcycle and makes his way over to New Jersey.

. . . .

John knocks on Sarah's door repeatedly until she answers.

She opens the door slowly, trying not to show any emotion, and keeps her eyes to the ground.

He can tell she's been crying from the bags underneath her eyes. "Sarah..."

"You have to go, John."

He tries to gently pick up her chin, but she moves her face away; she knows if she feels his touch, she'll melt right into his arms.

"You *have* to go, John," she repeats, staying firm and cold as stone.

"Sa—"

He tries to get a word in, but she steps back and shuts the door.

With the air taken from her, she sits with her back against the door, quietly weeping, knowing he stands heartbroken just inches from her. All she wants to do is hold him close, but she knows she'll only end up hurting more since he cannot stay.

Broken and torn in every way, John knows he must let her go for now; he loves her too much to cause her any more pain.

"I love you, Sarah," he chokes up. "I understand. It's too hard. I get it. I'll give you your space. But I *promise* you, I'm coming back home—and I'm coming back for you."

With his throat in knots, he places his hand on her door, hoping she'll somehow feel his love. And after a few moments of aching silence, and no more words to speak, he walks away.

"I love you too, John," she whispers, as she listens to the fading sound of his footsteps.

*   *   *   *   *
   *   *   *   *
*   *   *   *   *

Layla feels a sharp pain in her chest and stumbles to the ground. "What's . . . what's happening?" she asks the angels as she grabs at her chest.

They step away from her and look on with worry.

"Someone, someone help me. I can't feel anything," she pleads, stretching her hand out to them. But they make no move toward her; they only watch at a distance with heavy hearts. There's nothing they can do to save her. John and Sarah's destiny has taken a turn for the worst after Sarah shut him out of her life, which can only mean one thing: Layla can no longer exist.

The flickering light of John and Sarah's love has begun to die out, but not before the rest.

"Mom? Mom, what's happening?"

"Dylan? Dylan!" Layla shouts in horror, witnessing her son fade right before her eyes: if she seizes to exist, so will he and everyone after him.

One by one, John and Sarah's bloodline begins to fade away, yet Layla remains. Although her light flickers dim, she is spared, solely because of her father's promise to return for her mother.

But a promise is only a promise, no guarantee.

6
CHAPTER SIX

It has been weeks since the breakup, and although the days have come and gone, the despair Sarah felt that night has cemented in her heart. And that broken heart that now rests in her has gained full control and leads her down a dark path of self-destruction. She's changed her mentality toward the world; everything that she had ever believed in—or cared about—is no longer relevant. Her attitude has become sharp and unsympathetic, and her appearance accompanies her new way of thinking: she's dyed her beautiful long black hair to dark red, drowned herself in makeup and often wears tight clothing to show off her womanly figure. The once humble, hard-working, career-driven young woman that she was is now a freethinking, all-night binge-drinking party girl. She's out of control and headed down a path that is far less than she deserves, but no one around her can hear her cries for help through her false persona. The only ones around are Jenn and Casey, and they love the new Sarah. She's fun and spontaneous, finally the friend they've been waiting for.

IN THE EVENING OF A SCHOOL NIGHT, during what appears to be the start of a blizzard, John's in class taking a test when suddenly all of the long hours he'd spent studying fails him as he finds it hard to focus, not because of the strong blows of the wind crashing against the windowpanes but because Sarah runs through his mind, and he can sense something is very wrong.

Focus, *stay focused*, he tells himself, trying to fight his own paranoia. But fifteen minutes in, he places his pen down on his paper, grabs his bag and coat, and storms out of class.

The roads are too slushed and winds are too heavy to ride his bike, so he leaves it behind and opts to take the train.

. . . .

Sarah, Jenn and Casey are at Bar A flirting with many different men throughout the night until Sarah spots the man that lent her his phone a few months back and decides to make her way over to him.

"Hey, remember me?" She playfully winks at him as he quietly sips on his Jack and Coke.

"Oh, hey, the girl with the lost phone, Sarah, right?" he responds, scratching his head as if he hadn't been sitting there every Wednesday night waiting for her.

"Yes, sir," she confirms, flirtatiously touching his shoulder and blushing like a schoolgirl with a crush. "I didn't get your name."

"Lucas," he answers, eyeing her up and down.

"Ah, *Lucas*, finally a name to the face that's been running through my mind."

"Oh, really?"

She licks her lips. "Absolutely."

He chuckles.

"What's funny?"

"Do you believe in destiny?"

She rolls her eyes. "Ugh, no."

"Well, I do. You see, I tried to call, and even texted you, but I never got a response. When I didn't hear back from you, I told myself if you and I were meant to see each other again, we would. So I let it be, and here you are, once again."

"Coincidence, nothing more. And I didn't text or call you back because I had a boyfriend—" Sarah leans into his ear "—*had*."

Lucas smirks. "Does that mean you're going to let me buy you a drink this time?"

"Oh, yes . . . *many*."

"Well then"—he waves over at the bartender—"she'll have a raspberry martini, salted rim, chilled, with a twist of lime."

"Excuse me? You're not going to ask me what I'd like to drink? What kind of gentleman are you?" she jokes.

He leans into her ear and whispers, "Oh I can be gentle, but I know what you like and what you *really* want."

"Oh, do you?" she asks, egging him on to play this game, waiting for the right answer; she longs for a man's touch.

"Yes, here—" he hands her the martini "—was I wrong?"

She plays along and seductively takes a sip while keeping her eyes locked into his. "Mmm, it's delicious."

"I told you."

Lust boils from Sarah's eyes down into her bones as she itches for his touch. She runs her hand up his arm, and he grabs her by the waist and leans in for the kiss . . .

"Sarah," John speaks up, standing at a distance and trembling in his wet, disheveled clothes from the unforgiving blizzard.

She stops shortly from Lucas' venomous kiss, and her face turns white as if she's heard a ghost.

John walks over to her. "Let's go, Sarah," he demands, forcefully grabbing her hand.

"What are you doing?" She shoves his hand away from hers, not liking his approach. "I'm not going anywhere, John. What's wrong with you?"

John breathes deep, trying his best to keep his rage at bay, because the man that sits directly behind him (Lucas) is the same man he saw Sarah with in his dream. "Sarah, let's go," he demands once more, reaching for her hand.

"Did you not hear her? She's not going anywhere. Leave her alone," Lucas speaks up, holding back his smirk.

The sound of his voice burns a fire in John. And without hesitation, he turns around, knocks Lucas off of his seat and attacks him like a madman.

Lucas doesn't fight back. Instead, he allows John to beat on him because he knows that Sarah is a sucker for helpless people. And right now, John looks like the bully.

John kicks and punches Lucas relentlessly until the bouncers rush over and pin him to the wall.

"I know who you are!" he screams. "*I know who you are!!*"

Sarah rushes to Lucas' side and looks at John with pure disgust, as if she didn't know who he was anymore.

The bouncers grab John by his hands and feet and throw him out the front door, and he falls on his back into the snow. "You better go before we call the cops," they warn.

He picks himself up, wipes the slush from his clothes and looks through the stained glass window at Sarah tending to Lucas.

She feels his stare, stands and looks back at him. His pain-filled eyes pierce into hers, and the persona she's put on wants so desperately to die. Every part of her soul wants to run out to him, but she knows she must keep him at a distance or else her heart will break all over again, so she turns her back to him and runs into the bathroom.

John's heart shatters like hot water on cold glass. The love of his life has given up on him, yet again, and left him no choice but to walk away a defeated man.

He walks one mile through the storm to get to the train station, and the six inches of snow doesn't seem to affect him, nor does the blistering cold wind. He pays no mind to the physical pain his body is going through; all that he feels is heartache. It's as if his soul has been drained from his body, and he's now nothing more than a walking corpse.

Forty-five minutes later, he arrives at the station.

Instead of standing inside, where it's warm, he chooses to sit outside and endure the pain that the cold brings as he waits for his train. He sits slumped on the bench and doesn't budge an inch as the blusterous winds threaten to tear the very seat beneath him. Train after train comes and goes, but he does not board one. He can't find it in him to get up and leave, falsely hoping she'd come any minute. But when the last train of the night slowly pulls up to the station, John, once again, is left with no other choice but to leave a defeated man.

. . . .

"It's almost last call," says the bartender as John walks into his local bar at three in the morning.

"Well then, I guess I'll have to drink fast," he mutters.

"Rough night?"

He cynically chuckles, shakes his head and sits at the end of the bar.

The bartender gives him a shot and then another…and another, until he's so sloppy he can barely keep from falling off of the bar stool.

When the bar closes, John is forced to face reality and head home, alone.

He stumbles into his apartment, vomiting and falling over nearly all of his furniture in the living room until he inevitably lands flat on his back and is unable to get up. As he lies on the floor in his drunken state, his eyes scan the room, and he spots the source of all of his heartache: the academic books on his shelves. They symbolize everything that has taken Sarah away, all of the time that he has spent studying instead of being with her; but more importantly, on one shelf a book rests that once brought him inspiration and hope—the book that has been the source to all of his beliefs. He had once looked upon it with wondrous eyes, but not today. Today he views that Bible with the eyes of a serpent, reddened with hate and disgust. His eyes become fixated on the same gold lettering that once pulled him in, which is now wearing away from its many years of use and no longer has the same shine it once had. He's read that old passage, John 3:3, nearly every day in hope that his visions would come true, but now he's grown to hate everything about it.

With every bit of strength he has left, he manages to pick himself up and staggers his way over to his shelves. He then rips them from the walls and begins to destroy everything else around him.

Satan looks on and is humored by the fragile spirit of the human being. He laughs, points at John and looks up toward the heavens. "Your *great* creation, the *petty* human spirit. I told you they aren't worth any more than the dirt you'd risen them from!"

St. Michael appears in the opposite corner of the living room.

"Go ahead"—Satan gestures to John—"perform your miracles. I dare you to try, or does your master not allow you to? Tell me, when will you learn to speak your own thoughts, you *puppet*."

St. Michael stands stern and does not utter a word, dismissing Satan's ridicule.

Determined to be acknowledged, Satan assures his presence by walking toward St. Michael and standing right in front of him. He stares into his eyes like a chained lion with antelope just feet from him, eager to devour his beliefs. "He's mine. You and your god will see just how far the human loyalty stretches when they're put to the test. All of their prayers are but *temporary*. Once they aren't granted what is wished, their praise quickly turns into blasphemy. The human soul is foolish, but I guess it's fitting since they were made in the image of their creator."

St. Michael breaks his silence: "Do you believe that you can harm this man without the permission of the Father? All that you have done to John has only occurred because it has been permitted. You are but a tool for his will, nothing more."

Satan's eyes grow even more deathly, and he tries to intimidate St. Michael by placing his face inches from his.

St. Michael stares back, and continues, "I am not here to help this man. You need not worry. We have played this game once before. The LORD had given you Job, and you failed. Behold, here is John, another righteous man. God has given you permission to do as you please."

"I do not *need* permission. But if you are not here to save him, then what is your purpose?"

"To challenge you. You may throw everything you have at this man, and you will see that he will not fall. The *true* faithful human spirit is as an indestructible wall that cannot be brought down, no matter what you throw at it. Do all that you please to him, with no limitation." St. Michael then disappears.

"Oh, and I will," Satan chuckles, turning back around to revel in John's pain.

"Why!!" John shouts, breathing heavily and looking up as if he were speaking one on one with God. "Why me? Out of everyone in this world, why me? Why take away all that I love? Do I not deserve happiness? Have I not been a good person? What have I done wrong?" John's tears flood down his face. "There are people living in this world that deserve *nothing*, yet have everything. All of the happiness is theirs for the taking. But me, I'm left with nothing! Scum rule this world and you allow it! I choose to do the right things for the sake of being good and showing the world that good exist, but I don't know anymore... because I get nowhere. I get no help. Instead, you allow me to be tortured with visions of a life that I *can't* have! I've stepped into your church every Sunday of my life and followed every rule the best that I could, and *this* is where you put me? Down in the trenches like some unwanted child! Well I don't need y—" John pauses, catching himself.

Satan watches on like a giddy child waiting for candy as he waits for John to curse God's name.

John looks around at the mess he's created and is embarrassed by his behavior, and the animal he's become. "What have I done?" he sobs, falls to his knees, and weeps like a lost child seeking help.

Satan becomes enraged as John places guilt on himself rather than God, and decides to take a new approach: he walks behind John and whispers into his ear words that fill him with misery. John's mind begins to race, seeing no end to his suffering as Satan pushes him into the depths of darkness. The paranoia of losing his mind quickly overwhelms him, and he begins to shake uncontrollably.

He bows his head and pleads for mercy. "I'm sorry. Forgive me, Lord. I don't speak any truth, just the words of a weak, drunken man. Give me strength to continue, and I will."

"Noo!" Satan shouts.

St. Michael reappears, walks over to John, kneels and wraps his arms around him.

Feeling a sense of tranquility, John lies down next to the mess he's created and falls into a deep, peaceful sleep.

7

CHAPTER SEVEN

On a Friday night, while most students on campus are partying and living out their college dreams, John has his face buried in books inside his college library. He's taken the maximum amount of credits allowed each semester in order to speed up his graduation date and return to Sarah. But eighteen credits, a full-time job and the stress of losing the love of his life have proven to be too much. The visions of Sarah and Layla were once thoughts of inspiration, but they have now grown into a distraction that doesn't allow him to focus. No matter how hard he tries to succeed for them, it is the thought of losing them that cripples his progress.

I can't get this, he thinks, succumbing to the idea that he's just not cut out to be an architect. *I need to graduate, now. I can't waste any more time.*

John's eyes rim with tears of defeat when suddenly he hears a girl sobbing in the distance. He looks up, but no one is there.

It's not real, he tells himself, fearing his stress may be causing him to hallucinate. But her soft cries don't let up, and the gentleman in him doesn't allow him to stay seated, so he stands, looks around, and then makes his way through each aisle until he finally spots her.

There she sits, a breathtaking 19-year-old blonde with ocean blue eyes in a green dress, with her hands clinched together as tears flow from her pretty face.

"Are you okay?" he asks, relieved to know he wasn't going crazy, but also concerned for her.

"I'm fine," she whimpers, sniffling and wiping her tears away from her face. "I'm just having a hard time, that's all."

"I see."

"I've been studying for this *stupid* test for weeks, and I don't think I've learned a damn thing. It's all just a waste of time. My family will be *so* proud of me."

"Don't worry. I feel the same way. What's your major?"

"Architecture."

He chuckles.

"What's so funny?" she asks.

"We're in the same boat."

"Huh? I'm not following."

"I'm an architecture major, too—on academic probation. You see, we're both struggling. God help us if we graduate. Our homes will be like residential Tower of Pisas," he jokes, hoping to make her smile, and she does.

"Academic probation?"

"Yep, guilty."

She looks at him and raises her brow. "Well, I'm not drowning like you."

John laughs. "I'm John by the way."

"Nice to meet you, John. Eliana."

"Hey listen—" he scratches his head "—I don't want you to think I'm trying to pick you up or anything, but if you'd like to study with me, then maybe we can help each other."

She takes a good look at him and knows he's genuine. "I'd like that."

"Well then, let's go make these Pisas," John jokes again, helping her to her feet and picking up her books.

They spend the next three hours studying, joking and getting to know each other, and John can't help but take long glances at her in disbelief of how perfect she is, and she does the same. There's something angelic about her, almost unreal, dreamt up—and there's only one person he's felt that way about before.

The Librarian makes her way over to them. "Okay, guys, it's closing time. We'll be open at nine tomorrow."

For the first time, John wouldn't mind studying a little longer and neither would Eliana, but with no choice they gather their belongings and make their way outside.

John breaks the awkward silence. "Wow, it's freezing."

She nervously giggles in agreement as she shivers and rubs her arms.

"Well, uh, it was really nice studying with you, Eliana."

"Same here, John."

He reaches to shake her hand, but she goes in for a hug.

"See you around," he whispers, pulls back and begins to walk away.

"Hey, um..."

John turns around. "What's that?"

"I'm hungry. Do you, um, would you—"

"You want to get something to eat?"

"Well since you asked," she jokes, playfully fluttering her eyes at him.

He stops for a second and thinks it through. He knows he can't befriend her past tonight because his love's for Sarah.

"Eliana, I can't."

She pouts. "*Pretty please*, just a quick bite? Are you really going to make me eat alone?"

He knows exactly what she's doing, and the game she's playing, but he can't resist. "Fine, you win. Let's go eat."

. . . .

She's adorable, John thinks, as he sits across the table from Eliana and watches her eat. Everything she does is cute, even down to the way she nibbles on her food.

What's keeping him away? she asks herself, knowing that he likes her by the way he quietly stares.

There's an absolute spark between them, and no matter how hard John tries to stay emotionally distant, something keeps pulling him to her. For the past couple of hours, he's finally felt a sense of content, almost as if the burden he felt earlier was never there.

"Oh my God, is it really one in the morning!" Eliana shouts to her surprise. "That can't be right, is it?"

John grins knowing her time is correct as he recollects all of their different talks throughout the night about life, careers, love and philosophy—and he smiles knowing that he never grew tired for a second.

"We should probably get going, then. My bike is just two blocks from here. I can give you a ride home, if you'd like."

"I'd love that. I've never been on one before!"

. . . .

"I had a great time, thanks for everything. Who knew we'd meet, right?" Eliana smiles, and nervously twirls her hair as she leans on her front door. "The world works in mysterious ways."

John looks at her, absolutely drawn by her beauty. "In more mysterious ways than you'd think. Goodnight, Eliana."

"Hey, John . . ."

"Yeah?"

"Do you want to have another study session, soon?"

John's suddenly caught in a dilemma: he's learned so much with her help, so studying with Eliana would almost guarantee he'd pass—and in order to get back to Sarah, he must graduate—but he knows that too much time with Eliana can be dangerous.

"Well?"

He takes a moment, then answers, "Tuesday. Same time and place."

8
Chapter Eight

Tuesday has turned into Wednesday, Wednesday into Thursday, days into weeks and weeks into months. John and Eliana have seen each other nearly every day since they first met, and the inevitable has happened: he has fallen in love with her, and she with him. Life with Eliana feels easy, effortless—right. Yet, every so often, when the days die down and the night grows quiet, Sarah rules his mind.

Eliana wakes, feeling John's side of the bed empty, and turns on the bedside lamp, spotting him standing hunched over by the window as he quietly stares up at the sky.

"What's wrong, babe?" she asks, with a hoarse voice.

He doesn't answer.

"Babe?"

"I just can't sleep. Don't worry, go back to bed."

"What are you staring at?" she questions, sluggishly getting out of bed and making her way over to him.

"Nothing."

She wraps her arms around him, kisses his back and asks again, "What are you looking at? Show me."

"There aren't any stars out."

"It's the city. There's never any stars out," she laughs, biting his back. "Come on, let's go back to bed—" she grabs his hand and tries to persuade him to follow "—*please?*"

He doesn't budge. He just continues to stare at the night sky, remembering the story he once told Sarah about Layla being the brightest star.

"Come on, you can't stay up all night. We have the biggest test of our lives tomorrow. You need your rest. Come lie down with me."

Eliana's words die in the air as John's mind can only obsess over the love he's lost.

She finally lets go of his hand, sighs, and stands between him and the window, forcing him to look her in the eyes. "What is it?" she asks, although deep down she already knows; she's seen this desperation in his eyes one too many times.

"It's nothing. I'm fine, go back to bed."

"Just say it, John. I want to hear you say it."

He remains mute.

"Say it. Say her name."

He looks away, unable to gather the words.

Eliana tears and begins to breakdown, knowing their love was always temporary. "Every night—" she chokes up "—every night I lie next to a man who utters a name that isn't mine, and every night I pray that one day he'd utter mine instead. So get it over with already. Tell me it's over while you're awake. Don't make me lie next to a man that isn't mine."

"She's—"

"Your first love? I know. But I've been the one here, not her. While she took your love for granted, I danced in it."

John looks away, unable to look at her in pain.

"Look at me" —she grabs his face—"I see you stare at that calendar every day hoping that our graduation date would hurry up and get here, and every day I look away. But I can't look away anymore. You either come lie down with me or watch me walk out that door. So what's it going to be, John?

John caresses her face, wiping away her tears. "I care about you, Ellie, *so much*."

"But?"

"But I could never love you the way that I love her."

The air is taken from Eliana as she gasps in disbelief.

"I'm sor—"

"Don't. Don't say another word."

She walks past him, grabs her belongings and begins to pack a bag.

"It's the middle of the night. You can't leave now."

She doesn't respond.

He walks over and puts his hand over her bag. "Ellie, stop."

"*Move*, John."

"You can't go out at this time. It's dangerous."

She removes his hand from her bag and makes her way toward the door. But before leaving, she stops and looks back at John. "You don't have to be that guy, you know. You don't have to be her knight in shining armor. You can't force love, John, and that's why I'm leaving. I love you, I *really* do, but you need to learn how to love me and *only* me."

She closes the door, and John is left feeling emptier than ever as he walks back over to the window and desperately stares up at the sky, hoping Sarah is doing the same.

9

CHAPTER NINE

"You're terrible for me," Sarah groans, blowing smoke out of her mouth as she slides her naked body off of Lucas.

"Yet, you're still here," he growls.

"I had a future before, a bright future, until I met this gorgeous face of yours." She grabs his face and kisses him as smoke pours out from her mouth and fills his lungs.

"You had nothing more than a dream, a false dream, like everyone else. But I saved you from that lie. I saved you from worthless hours of study and overwhelming debt from student loans that you'd be paying back until the day you die. I showed you the truth about this world. Nobody cares about a degree, only what you can do for them. And you, my beauty, can do it *all*." He grabs her face and kisses her. "Isn't this what everyone dreams of?" He takes a pull of a joint and grabs her by her hips, pulling her close. "Love, sex and drugs. What else can you ask for? Everyone screams your name day in and day out. They lust for you, daydream and fall asleep thinking about you."

"I guess so," she responds, turning to her side and staring out the window. "But, sometimes, I feel like there can be more."

"What are you looking at?" he questions, kissing her shoulders.

"What my life would've been like if I'd kept following that dream."

"Dreams are nothing more than *dreams*. They're elusive, unobtainable—unrealistic. But if you really want to dream, this right here can make you dream the greatest of dreams." He places a bag of heroin in front of her. "It will take you away for hours on end and place you wherever you wish to be. All of the colors and mysteries of the world will come rushing into your mind with one hit, and you'll dream like never before."

"I told you, I don't do that kind of drug. I'm no junky."

Lucas becomes irritated. "What are you talking about? You'll snort a line off of a mule's ass if you had the chance. Drugs are drugs. If you want to dream so fucking badly, then this will make you dream."

"That won't take me there. Nothing can, not anymore," she whispers to herself.

"What did you say?"

She ignores him, gets out of bed and walks over to the window. "I said *nothing*, not you or any drug, can take me there." She places her hand on the glass and outlines the stars with her finger. "I can never get there, not anymore."

"Come back to bed."

"For what? Why do you even bother with me?"

"Because I love you," Lucas lies, walking over to her. He then kisses her shoulder and rubs her back.

"Please don't touch me..."

"Your high is crashing that's why you're so emotional right now. You have to hit this. Don't you want to feel better?"

"I'm. No. Junky."

"So what are you going to do? Are you going to cry all fucking night? There's nowhere else to go. You just said that, didn't you? Where exactly is it that you want to go, anyway? You want to go home, back to your ungrateful family?" Lucas walks over to the nightstand and grabs his phone. "Here, call your family."

Sarah's eyes redden.

"What's wrong? Oh, that's right, not even your family wants you. Tell me, what is it that your mother told you when you called her on the holidays?"

Sarah's lips quiver as she shakes beneath her skin.

"What did she say! You don't remember? Well, let me remind you. She said she doesn't know who you are, but you are no daughter of hers. Is that where you want to go? Back to a place that no longer loves you? You're damaged goods to them."

Sarah shakes her head.

"No? Then why are you acting like this?"

She tries to hold back her tears.

Lucas grabs her face, digging his nails into her skin. "Don't you cry."

"I'm sorry."

"I don't want to hear sorry. Don't you *ever* disrespect me again."

"I won't, I promise. It's the drugs. You know how I get when I need more. I was just thinking too much, that's all."

"And what exactly were you thinking about?" Lucas presses, knowing it was John.

"Nothing... my, my mind is foggy."

"I don't believe you." He places his forehead on hers, grabs her by the throat and looks deep into her eyes. "Don't you lie to me."

"I'm not. I was just coming down from my high, and it made me think about my life—in a stupid way. Believe me, I'm so grateful for all that you've given me. You are my *king*, no one else." She knows just the right words to calm his anger, and the devil in him is instantly pleased. "Give me that." She points to the needle sitting on the nightstand. "If I'm going to do this, at least let me do it alone."

He walks over to the nightstand, grabs the needle and hands it to her.

"Alone," she repeats.

He nods and sits at the corner of their bed to give her space.

She pulls a chair up to the window, wraps her arm with an old t-shirt and slowly pierces her skin. The heroin quickly takes control and her body tweaks.

As the high invades her soul, she sees a shooting star across the sky and reaches out for it.

"John," she whispers before passing out.

10
Chapter Ten

The Dean announces John's name to receive his degree at the podium. "John Harper, Bachelor of Arts and Architecture."

John doesn't hear his name being called because he's too preoccupied scanning the audience.

The Dean clears his throat. "Bachelor of Arts and Architecture, *John Harper*."

John finally snaps out of it and makes his way up the steps. But as he is honored for his achievement, he stands looking dejected into the audience. Although he has many supporters, family and close friends, clapping and cheering for him, he doesn't find Sarah standing in the crowd as he'd always thought she would. The audience roars as they watch him tear up, thinking his glassy eyes come from his proud sense of accomplishment, but they only flow from heartache.

After the ceremony, John goes out to dinner with his family.

"John, we're all so proud of you. You did it! You stuck it out and really made something of yourself!" says his mother.

He forces a smile on his face. "Thank you, guys. Thanks for showing up."

"We saw you looking everywhere. I don't know how you didn't see us. We were yelling so loud," says his father, Jim.

"I don't know. I guess the place was so loud and packed that I couldn't tell where you all were."

"So, are you excited for the future? What are you going to do next? You have any jobs lined up?" asks Rosa, his aunt.

"Yeah, actually, I do. I got a job opportunity in California. I think I'll live out there for a while, get my life in order, experience new things then, eventually, come back," he answers, knowing the only reason he's taking the job in California is because Sarah's there. He knows this through friends back home. Every now and then he'd find a way to ask how she was or where she was living. But no one could ever tell him the truth about her, fearing it would crush him, so they lied and told him that she transferred to UCLA and was working just as hard as he was in pursuit of her own career. This comforted him throughout his hardships and kept him going.

Gabe, John's younger brother, by two years, throws his fork on the table in disgust.

"What's wrong?" John asks.

Gabe clinches his jaw. "Nothing. Nothing's wrong."

"You're obviously upset about something."

Gabe bites his tongue and remains silent.

"Gabe, what's wrong?"

Everyone stares at Gabe with wide eyes, hoping he wouldn't spill the beans.

"Gabe, if you have something to say, just say it. No one's going to throw you a pity party."

"It's nothing, just...just leave it alone." Gabe pushes his chair back, gets up and walks outside for some air, but John doesn't let up and follows him out.

"Hey! What's your problem, man?"

Gabe turns around and walks up to him. "You. You're my problem. Better yet, you *have* a problem."

John takes a step back. "What are you...what are you talking about? What problem do I have?"

"You're obsessed, John. Let her go, *please*. I'm begging you. I know that's the only reason why you're going out there. You have a good thing going for you here. Don't mess it up like you did with Eliana. *Move on*."

"You don't understand, Gabe, and I don't expect you to. But this is *my* life, and I need her in it. I'm coming back home, don't worry."

"No, *you* don't understand, John. You *really* don't."

"What don't I understand? Tell me. She's my love, my *true* love, and I know it for a fact even though I can't explain it to you—I just know. You're going to have to trust me on this one. One day, you're going to meet a girl and understand exactly how I feel. She's going to brighten your day and put your mind at ease, and just the simple thought of her is going to give you the greatest joy you've ever had."

Gabe's not buying it. "You guys dated years ago. You both were children. It's time to move on, John—she obviously has."

"You don't know that."

"John, look, she's—" Gabe stops himself.

John's blood boils, and he grabs Gabe by the collar. "She's what?"

"What are you going to do? You're going to hit me? You'll fight your own blood for some girl? Then *hit me*. Go ahead, *hit me*." Gabe picks his chin up, and John comes to his senses. He lets Gabe go, knowing he could never hurt his brother, and walks away.

"Tell Mom and Dad I said bye. I don't have an appetite anymore, thanks to you."

"She's not the dream girl you think about, John. She's far from it! You need to wake up to reality. WAKE UP!"

John stops dead in his tracks as if he's heard a ghost when those specific words ring in his ears and trigger him to remember his first dream, when his own image told him to wake up from the delusion of life and love.

With bated breath, he turns around and walks toward Gabe. "What did you say?"

"She's not the trophy wife you think she is, John. She's a—" Gabe pauses again, trying to figure out how to tell his brother the truth.

"Choose your words wisely, little brother."

Gabe witnesses a side of John he's never seen before: his eyes reddened in anger as if something has taken over him; he looks crazed and sick.

John's voice heightens and nostrils flare. "If you have something to tell me, you better tell me now. No more games."

"She's a stripper and a drug addict."

John's brows lower. "What are you talking about?"

"I told you, John. She's not this fantasy girl you're constantly dreaming about. She's a drug-addicted stripper. And I'm sorry that I'm the only one with the balls to break the news to you but you're my older brother, my hero. I can't let you live another second of this lie. You deserve to know the truth."

John's world begins to spin upside down. "You're lying."

"I'm not. I swear to you. You know I wouldn't. Everyone knows. Ever since she moved out to Cali with her boyfriend, her life has turned to shit. Even her own family disowned her."

"How could you keep this from me?"

"We—"

"We knew if we told you, you would quit school and try to rescue her like you're Superman and she's Lois Lane," John's father intervenes, walking toward them. "We knew the idea of winning her back was the driving force behind you finishing school. And as long as she was out there doing well, you would stay focused in your studies. But the time has come for you to know the truth, and accept it. I'm sorry you couldn't have the happy ending you've dreamt about for so long, but you have so much to offer any other girl. You're a handsome, brilliant young man with a heart bigger than anyone I've ever met. Any girl would dream to be with a guy like you. It's time to move on, John. It's time to start a new life." Jim tries to put his arms around John to console him, but he wants no part of it.

"Get off of me!" John shrugs him off and takes several steps back. "Do you think it's okay keeping this from me? It's not up to you or *anyone* to decide what I do with my life. You're not allowed to play God."

"Son . . . "

"I'll see you around." John turns his back on both of them and runs to his bike.

"What's going on?" Gail asks as she walks outside wondering what's taking them so long.

John speeds off.

"Nothing. Go back inside, honey," Jim answers, escorting her back through the revolving doors.

They all return to their table, and everyone eats their dinner in silence; no one wants to be the first to bring up the elephant in the room.

"I'm sorry, but are we really just going to sit here and eat like nothing's wrong? He's sick, guys. There's something wrong with your son. He needs help, and he needed it yesterday," Gabe lets out. "His eyes...you should've seen the way he looked at me. It's the same look that your brother has today and the same look that your father had three years ago. He ended up killing himself. Is that what you want for your son?" he asks his mother.

She shakes her head, tearing up.

"Then help him, Mom. I'm begging you, *please*. Help your son."

Gail covers her face with her napkin and starts to weep. She knows Gabe is right but doesn't want to face the reality that her boy might be troubled.

Jim slams his fist on the table. "Apologize to your mother, right now! There's nothing wrong with him. For God's sake, he just graduated college. He's fine!"

"I'm sorry, Dad, but your son is crazy and needs help. He needs to be medicated."

Jim's never laid a hand on any of his children, but Gabe is coming close to being the first.

"Um, I don't mean to interrupt, but what are you guys talking about?" asks Adam, John's best friend. "And where's John?"

Jim exhales. "He left. He just found out the truth about Sarah, and his entire world has been turned inside out. He's heartbroken, like any other man would be. He'll get over it, though. It's just going to take some time."

"Oh man," Adam gasps, leaning back in his chair.

"What?" Gabe asks.

"Really? You guys didn't put it all together? Where do you think John's headed right now?"

Everyone's heart drops, realizing John is headed straight to *California*.

11

CHAPTER ELEVEN

JOHN RACES TOWARD JFK AIRPORT without any concern for his own safety as he flies by other vehicles on the dark highway road. Although he's en route to the airport, he's still indecisive on what to do. Does he take his family's advice and forget about Sarah, risking the loss of true love, or does he have faith and chase his destiny?

With less than five miles to the airport, he panics and takes the next exit and then rents a motel room for the night.

Two weeks later, he's still in that room.

With the shades drawn and only a small lamp lit by his bedside, he spends all of his time thinking. He doesn't shave, shower or go outside unless he needs to eat—and even then it's to the vending machine in the lobby.

Most days he paces back and forth, tortured by the thought of her new lifestyle, and places blame on himself for it all: he wasn't there for her when she pleaded for him, but instead ignored her need for love in his quest for success. Other days, he's furious at her for giving up on him after all he's given up for her.

Eventually he breaks. True love or no true love, dreams or no dreams, he must move on with his life. Sarah's no longer the girl he once knew, so his true love no longer exists; but there's one girl that has never turned her back on him, and he makes plans to call her in the morning.

"Stop, John!!" Sarah laughs as he chases her through the woods in the snow.

"I'm coming for you!" he shouts, jumping over logs of fallen trees, and tackles her into nature's white powder.

"Get off of me," she giggles.

He climbs on top of her and playfully kisses every part of her face, and then stops to take in the moment. He looks deep into her eyes as if she holds his entire life in them.

"I'm never going to let you go."

She smiles, comforted by his words, and looks back into his eyes in the same way. "I hope not," she responds, arching her back and picking up her chin to kiss him. But before her lips can meet his, she disappears.

Alone and confused, John remembers his recent decision to let her go and is now left to face his new reality: a cold life without her.

"Sa—"

"—Sarah," John whispers, waking himself.

Although he's now awake, he can still smell her sweet perfume and feel the warmth of her body for a few more seconds until it finally fades and he's left to lie in a humid motel room that's filled with his own body's stench.

He turns over and sits at the corner of the bed, as he's done for weeks on end, and pulls out his wallet from his front pocket. He opens it and takes out an old picture of him and Sarah that very moment they kissed in the snow. She had taken it herself.

Everything was so clear the night before, but now the vicious cycle of uncertainty continues as he's tortured once again, no longer by visions of a past life but of a life just a few years ago—when everything was bliss and everything was certain, when life was easy and hope ran thick.

He places the photo down on his bed and picks up his cell from the nightstand. He looks back at the picture once more and then makes the most important call of his life.

"Good afternoon, thank you for calling CBA Home Designs. How may I direct your call?"

"Hi, can I speak to Mr. Wallace, please?"

"I'm afraid he's in a meeting at the moment. Can I take a message or forward you to his voicemail?"

"It's really important. He's been waiting for my call. Would you mind telling him that John Harper is on the line?"

"Sure, one moment, please."

The receptionist puts him on hold and walks over to the conference room.

"Sorry to bother you, sir. I know you said to hold all calls but a gentleman named John Harper, on line 3, says it's important."

Mr. Wallace smirks, hoping to hear good news. "Not a problem, Cindy. I'll take it, thank you."

"Gentlemen, please excuse me for a moment. This is the kid I was talking to you about."

He walks away to take the call and answers the phone with enthusiasm in his voice. "*John Harper.*"

"Hello, sir."

"Please, call me Anthony."

"Okay. Hello, Ant.,"

"Attaboy! Now let's cut straight to the chase, Johnny. Are you in or are you out?"

John takes a moment and a deep breath, knowing he's about to make the biggest decision of his life. "Well, sir, there was a lot to consider, and I have to choose a place that feels like home to me."

"And is CBA Home Designs that place, John?"

John clears his throat. "It is. It's the only place I ever want to be. It's time to start a new chapter in my life."

"Well, welcome home, Johnny. You've chosen wisely. And as I had promised you in my proposal, I'll have a corporate apartment and a vehicle ready for you when you arrive. I see big things in the future for you and I, and I'm excited for it! When can you start?"

"Immediately."

"Perfect. I'll forward you back to Cindy. She'll get all of your information and e-mail you a ticket. Someone will be waiting for you when you arrive to take you to your new place. Be sure to pack light, John. California is hot."

. . . .

John's plane lands at LAX the next morning.

"Mr. Harper?"

"Yes? That's me."

"My name is Timothy. I'll be your chauffeur for the day, young man."

"Oh"—John extends his hand—"nice to meet you."

Timothy shakes his hand and bends down to grab his luggage.

"Where are we going?"

"I was told to bring you to your new place. It's only a few miles from here, about a twenty to thirty-minute car ride—depending on traffic."

John gets into the corporate limo.

"So, I hear you're from New York," asks Timothy.

"No, just went to school there. I'm from Jersey."

"Well, California is a big change from either of them. I hope you don't get homesick."

"This is my home now," John responds, thinking about Sarah. As long as he's with her, home can be anywhere. "Sir..."

"Yes, young man?"

"Would you mind..."

"Would I mind?"

"Would you mind showing me around before bringing me home?"

"Not at all. Do you have anywhere specific you'd like to go?"

John scratches his head, not knowing how to ask. "Are there any gentlemen's clubs around here?"

"It's a bit early in the morning. The women... how can I say this? The women are of a different 'class' at this hour. I recommend going later on tonight, but if that's what you want then so be it."

"No, I don't necessarily want to go in one right now. I just want to know of any around the area."

"Well, alright, I'll swing by a couple of popular places and give you a little tour of the city while we're at it. How does that sound?"

"That sounds perfect, sir. Thank you."

Timothy gives John a tour around the city, and he takes note of all the possible places Sarah might be. After the tour, Timothy brings him to his new apartment.

"What do you think?" asks Timothy as he opens the front door.

John's eyes can't believe what he's seeing. He's never been in such a luxurious place, let alone live in one. "It's—"

"Grande, isn't it?"

"—too much. I can't afford this."

"Ah, this is but one of the many perks of working for CBA. This building is owned by the corporation and houses many of its employees."

Timothy hands John his lease.

He looks at Timothy suspiciously. "No rent?"

"Free of charge, Johnny. All of this is part of the many perks, like Timothy said, of working for our company. As well as this," answers Anthony Wallace, John's new boss, as he walks out of the kitchen and opens a closet full of suits in the foyer.

Mr. Wallace walks up to John and extends his hand. "It's our pleasure to have you on board. If you work hard and do good by our company, you'll continue to have all of this"—he spreads his arms wide, showcasing the apartment—"and even more."

John shakes his hand with the firmest grip. "This is too much."

"Our company believes in our employees. We've built most of this city's landscape through the philosophy that if we spoil you, you'll spoil us with great work."

John exhales in disbelief. "I—"

"I'm glad you like it, Johnny." Mr. Wallace taps him on the shoulder and signals Timothy to leave with him. "We'll see you on Monday."

Still speechless, John simply nods as they walk out.

Once the door is locked behind him, he walks throughout his new home, and is amazed by its size and elegance. But when he walks outside onto the balcony, which overlooks the cityscape, he can't help but wonder where his love might be.

Nothing else matters anymore, not his new lavish apartment, nor the expensive suits or any of the other out-of-this-world amenities that came into his life. None of it. Nothing can ever fill the void of her love.

He reaches into his pocket and takes out the photo of him and Sarah in the snow, and stares at it for a few moments, thinking about what she might look like now. Many other thoughts rush through his mind, as well: Will he even be able to find her? And if he does, how will she handle it? Will she welcome him with an embrace or deny him like the last time? Does she even think about him anymore?

He knows there's no way to answer these questions, but he can't stop tormenting himself. There's only one way to find out. And even though finding her is a long shot in this big city, he's going to give it his all.

. . . .

She could be anywhere, he thinks, overwhelmed by the noise from the cars' horns honking in traffic and the loud music joined by the blinding, rhythmic lights from the clubs around him. It all becomes too much to handle. The fear of never finding Sarah is much more than unsettling; it's more of a reality than anything. He's searched for her day and night for weeks, and not once has he felt like he's had a good lead.

In an attempt to calm himself, he sits on a curb and rests his head down into the palms of his hands. As he's faced down, taking deep breaths, a flyer floats and lands directly beneath his feet, it reads:

LOVESHACK – GENTLEMEN'S CLUB

There's something about this flyer that draws him, but then again, his gut instinct hasn't been the best of friends lately. It's only a few blocks from where he is, a five-minute drive, so he decides to make the trip.

He arrives at a dingy, run-down, small, secluded place in the shadows of the rest of the high-end gentlemen's clubs. The atmosphere is filled with suffocating second-hand smoke, glue-like floors and countertops from spilt alcohol, and old perverted men throwing their money away, hoping to get lucky.

"Hello there, handsome," says a stripper, who walks up to John and tries to entice him by brushing her body up against his side.

He dismisses her and keeps his eye out for Sarah.

"You want a dance?" she asks, eager to service him; a man of his age and style doesn't come around very often.

"No thanks, maybe some other time."

He steps away from her and walks toward the bar.

"What would you like, honey?"

"A shot of Jameson and a Stella, please."

"Here you go, doll." The bartender seductively leans on the counter. "If there's anything else you need, let me know."

He smirks and shakes his head. "That'll be all, thank you."

Another dancer comes up to him, and then another, and another...and another. From his appearance, they see money.

He takes the opportunity to ask each of them if they know of a girl named Sarah, but none do. Not a single girl in the club knows of her, but they suggest that he stay and wait for the next shift of girls to come in.

He waits another two hours, watching each dancer come on and off the stage, but none are her. He's now ready to call it quits.

As he reaches into his pocket to give the bartender a tip, the music changes and the crowd suddenly goes wild.

"Gentlemen, are you ready!" the host booms.

It's been loud the past few hours, but there's something different about the cheers this time. It seems like they've been waiting for this moment all night.

John asks the bartender to change a fifty.

The host continues, "Well, take out all of your money! Rush to the ATM if you have to! Do whatever it takes to keep the money flowing and this beauty on stage!"

The crowd whistles as the drum roll begins.

"Gentlemen, the moment you've all been waiting for has finally arrived. Get on your feet and help me welcome our girl next door. The one and only...AMBER!!"

The crowd cheers, claps, and stomps on the ground so hard the floorboards vibrate. And John joins in, clapping softly as he waits for the bartender to bring back his change.

Out from the back, walking slowly and seductively, Amber arrives on stage.

John freezes in place, no longer entertained by the roars of the crowd. He's never met Amber before, but he knows that face from anywhere.

"Sarah?" he gasps.

Drugged up on cocaine and liquor, Sarah doesn't notice John sitting just a few yards from her.

Once the music dials down, and everyone sits back in their seats, John stands.

And even though his new corporate look is worlds from the young, broke college student he once was, she could never mistake the love of her life and those piercing eyes of his that see straight through her. She gasps and immediately tries to cover herself.

Although she desperately wants to run away, she can't seem to escape his stare. Those eyes that once looked upon her with pure admiration and love have now become full of dread.

Locked into each other's eyes, they both stand frozen in place with lips that utter silent, broken words.

She tears, and his eyes build up as he slowly walks toward her.

She shakes her head, pleading for him to stop, because even though her love for him remains, she knows she's lost who she once was and is no longer the girl he once loved, or known.

He doesn't listen and continues to walk toward her.

"No, John," she chokes up, unable to find a voice.

He's too far to hear her words but can read her lips clearly. Still, he continues to walk.

"No. Stay there," she cries out, raising her hand to make it clear.

He continues to walk.

"Stay away!" she shouts.

The music dies out, and everyone stares at John.

He stretches out his trembling hand. "Sarah, come with me. You don't belong here."

She frantically shakes her head and claws at her skin like an addict. "I can't," she sobs, struggling to catch her breath.

"You don't belong here. Please, come with me."

The pressure soon becomes too much, and she runs to the back of the stage.

He goes to chase, but is stopped by security.

"Let her go," they warn.

But he came too many miles, searched too many days, waited too many years and loved her for far too long to give up now. He tries to shove his way through them, screaming out for her, "Sarah!"

John's left security no choice but to throw him out, and they do so with ease. They toss him in the alley, and he lands flat on his back.

The door shuts, music turns back on, and the place goes wild again.

Sarah remains backstage as her promoter heckles at her to get back to work, but the sound of John's cry torments her as it plays over and over again in her head.

Lying flat on his back in an alley, John screams beneath his breath. He closes his eyes and takes three deep breaths to calm the rage that wants to explode within when suddenly he hears the sound of stilettos hitting the pavement.

"Are you okay?" Sarah asks, kneeling beside him.

He opens his eyes in disbelief, sits up and touches her face to make certain he's not dreaming.

She moves away from his touch, feeling dirty. All that she wants is for him to know that she cares, even if it is only for this one moment. She's ready to live out the rest of her damaged life and free him from it. "Go home, John."

"Go home?"

"Yes, go home. This isn't a place for you."

"And it is for you? Sarah, you know I'm not leaving here without you."

"You're going to have to," she responds, standing back on her feet and looking down at him. "Goodbye, John."

She turns her back and walks away as quickly as she can.

"You're good at that you know!"

She stops, keeping her back to him. "Good at what?"

"Running. Giving up. That's all you ever do. You can stop now. You don't need to run anymore."

She turns to face him. "Maybe that's what you should do. Run, John. Run away. Run far away from me."

She turns back around and continues to walk away.

John picks himself up and runs up to her, and she steadily walks past him, hiding her tears with her clutch, until he jumps in front of her and puts a halt to her steps.

"It's okay, we can go back home now. Come with me. It's that simple."

She remains silent, not budging an inch.

"I flew across the country to find you. *Please*, speak to me—at least look at me."

Her hands fall hopelessly to her sides, but she still continues to look at the ground in shame.

"Leave me," she weeps, with quivering lips and running mascara.

"I will never leave you, sweetheart. I love you, no matter what. I don't care about what you did. I don't need to know *anything*. I know *you*, and that's all I care about." He points at her heart. "That's all I need to know. All I want is you today, tomorrow and every day after. Yesterday doesn't matter. Will you, *please*, come home with me? I'll leave my job, change my career. I'll do whatever it takes to bring you back home."

"I can't just pick up my things and leave like that. I'm a different person now. You don't understand."

"I know you more than you think, and love you much more than you could *ever* understand."

John takes out his smartphone.

"What are you doing?" Sarah asks nervously.

"I'm going to be at LAX, Terminal 5, one week from today. The flight leaves at 5:30 p.m." He shows her the tickets' confirmation on his phone. "Come home with me."

"But—"

"One week from today."

Sarah's speechless. It's all just too much for her, but she agrees with a nod.

"It's going to be okay." He gently wipes the running mascara from her eyes. "Everything will be like it was. One day, all of this will become nothing more than an old nightmare. You trust me, right?"

She looks at him deeply, knowing he has been the only man she has ever trusted. "I do."

"Come on, let me take you home."

Sarah's eyes widen. "No, you can't."

"Why not?"

"You just can't. I don't—I don't want Lucas to see us together."

"He won't. I'll let you out a block from your place, just tell me when we're close. I promise."

He prays that she agrees, not only to make sure she's home safe but also to see where she's living.

"You promise?"

"I promise."

John takes the longest route to Sarah's house in order to spend every possible minute that he can with her. She doesn't say much during the ride, only compliments him on his success as she fidgets in her seat, needing her fix. He doesn't say much, either. The thought of her leaving weighs heavy on his heart, and it's all he can think about; no words can express the pain he feels knowing she sits just inches from him yet cannot stay.

After a half-hour drive, he stops one block from her home, puts the car in park and looks out of his driver-side window, because watching her leave would be too much to bear. "I'll see you in a week," he chokes up.

She sits in silence for a moment and then looks over at him. "John..."

He looks over at her.

"I can't do it," she confesses, grabbing his face and kissing him. "Just a little longer," she whispers, placing her hand on the cars gear stick and shifting it forward.

John grabs her face and intensely kisses her back as he puts his foot on the gas and drives off with the love of his life.

. . . .

They arrive at John's place and slowly begin to make love. They thirst for one another like two fish out of water yet take their time loving every part of each other's body. And although Sarah has been with many men over the years, none have made her feel the way John does. She feels protected and adored every time he touches her. All of the drugs and alcohol she'd consumed throughout her years of addiction were only mere substitutes for the love she's longed for. And now that she's finally in his arms again, she's the highest she's ever been.

Their passion lasts for hours into the night until they're so physically drained they can do nothing more than sleep.

John's standing in the middle of Terminal 5 at LAX as people swarm past him to board their planes.

He hears the announcement for his flight over the intercom: "Flight to Newark airport will be departing in fifteen minutes."

"Are you ready to—"

He looks to his left and Sarah's not there. The traffic in the terminal suddenly increases, and everyone begins to bump into John as they walk past him.

He pays little mind to them and only focuses on finding Sarah as he scrambles through the suffocating crowd, turning around anyone that resembles her from the back.

"Flight to Newark airport will be departing in five minutes."

Panic sets in. "Sarah!"

"I'm here, baby!" she shouts, and John's heart begins to beat again.

He turns around and spots her through the crowd, but realizes she's not looking back at him. The crowd then splits, and everyone turns around to stare at him.

The noise around him is drowned out by the giggles of a young boy, who runs into Sarah's arms.

"Babe, I've got the tickets. Let's hurry before our plane leaves," says Lucas, as he picks up the child and kisses her.

"Are you excited, Jake?" she asks, clapping her hands in excitement.

"Yes, Mommy!"

The three walk away with their backs turned to John, but Lucas turns his head and winks at him.

John closes his eyes, refusing to see any more. *This is a dream. This. is. just. a. dream.*

Over the intercom plays a conversation he and Sarah had that night on the shore:

"What if we had a son?" she asked.

"I don't think we will," he answered.

"Come on, I picked out our girl's name. Now it's your turn to pick out our boy's...Ugh, fine. I'll choose one myself. How about Jake?"

"She's mine," Satan's voice echoes into John's ears. "Just because you had her last night, doesn't mean she's there to stay."

The crowd points at John and joins in on Satan's laughter. "Hahah—"

"—ahaha!" laughs the host of the morning-radio show playing on John's alarm clock.

He wakes to sweat all over his chest and back as he breathes deeply. Thank God it's just a dream, he thinks, as he turns to check on Sarah.

She's gone.

12
Chapter Twelve

Sarah's cab pulls up in front of her house. She steps out, takes a deep breath and prays Lucas isn't waiting up for her. If ever there was a time she wished he didn't come home, last night was it.

With her fingers crossed, she walks up her steps and opens the door as quietly as she can.

"Where have you been?" Lucas asks, tapping his fingers around his coffee mug, as he sits in the kitchen waiting for the lie she's about to tell.

"At work. Where else?"

"Are you really going to stand there and tell me that you've been at the club for—" he looks at the clock "—eighteen hours? Do you take me as a fool?"

"You? No, I was the fool. I was a damned fool to think that a man like you could ever love me—or love, period. All you ever wanted was to *own* me, but I'm not yours. And yes, if you must know, that's *exactly* where I was. I was blowing one of your favorite clients you like to sell me to." She spits and throws a client's business card in his direction. "Maybe you should give him a call and charge him extra."

Lucas flips the table and she immediately tries to run back out the door, but he's too quick and grabs her by the hair and slams her face against the wall. "You little bitch!" he screams, spitting and foaming out of the mouth, and grabs her by the throat. "I know you were with him!"

Sarah's dazed, barely conscious, and bleeding profusely through her nose.

He drags her up the stairs by her shirt, and it rips and tears with every step. Halfway up the stairs her shirt finally shreds, and he's forced to pick her up.

He brings her to their room, throws her on the bed, and then ties her up to it and begins to rape her silent body until she wakes beneath him.

She pleads for him to stop, but he only feeds off of her cries each time she shouts for help.

"You think I don't know about your plan?" he whispers into her ear. "I have eyes *everywhere*. You're not going *anywhere*. I hope you enjoy being tied up like a pig for the rest of your fucking life!" He laughs. "You know what? I guess you were right. I *do* own you."

. . . .

John nervously paces back and forth in Terminal 5 as he waits for Sarah.

He hears the announcement for his flight over the intercom: "Flight to Newark airport will be leaving in the next fifteen minutes. Please have your tickets ready before boarding your plane."

"Come on, Sarah. Where are you?"

John can barely contain himself as the time seems to speed up, yet she's still nowhere in sight.

"Flight to Newark airport will be leaving in the next five minutes."

"I'm here, baby!"

John's heart stops, and he turns around.

A woman of Sarah's likeness kneels down and tickles her child.

He's frozen in place, hoping it's not her.

She looks up and he exhales, relieved that she isn't Sarah.

"Flight to Newark airport will be departing shortly. Please begin boarding your plane."

John has seconds to make a decision: Does he board without her and give up on their love, or does he wait a little longer in hope that she's just running late?

Three hours later, she still hasn't shown.

"Flight to Newark airport will be leaving in the next five minutes. Please have your tickets ready before boarding your plane."

John has no other choice but to leave her behind. His belief in destiny has proven to be false, and his entire life has become nothing more than one long, extended delusion that he cannot allow to continue.

As he walks through the jetway, he's held up in traffic. Everyone is moving extremely slow and it's beginning to irritate him. All he wants to do is board that plane, head home and never look back.

What the hell is taking so long? he thinks, as he tries to look over the shoulders of those in front of him. There seems to be some commotion at the front of the line.

"McKayla? McKayla, where are you!" screams a man, frantically walking in and out of the plane.

The flight attendants seem worried as well, and everyone in line looks around themselves.

"What's going on?" John asks the gentleman in front of him.

"A father lost his—"

"Daddy! Daddy, I'm here!" a four-year-old girl let's out, giggling innocently as if she were playing hide-and-seek.

Her father races to her, lifts her up and hugs her tight.

Everyone's heart grows warm, even John manages to smile, and the line finally starts to move.

Row 8, seat C, is where John sits waiting for everyone else to board. Next to him are McKayla and her father.

McKayla smiles at John and waves. "Hello!"

John smiles back. "Hi."

"Why are you sad?" she asks.

"McKayla!" warns her father. "I'm sorry about that, sir."

"It's okay."

"I'm sorry about the hold up, as well. I looked away for *one* second, and she just ran off."

"It's fine."

"She can be a handful at times. But I tell you, I'd go to the ends of the earth in search for her. You have any kids?"

John's world stops as the cries of Layla ring through him: "Daddy, please!! Don't let Mommy go!"

"Layla," John whispers to himself. "Hold that door!" he shouts at the flight attendant who's shutting the airplane's hatch.

"Sir, please sit down. We are about to takeoff any minute."

"I have to leave."

"I'm sorry, sir. I have specific orders from the captain to seat everyone and get ready for takeoff. No one can leave this plane without his approval."

John thinks of a quick lie. "I'm not feeling well. I think I still have the flu. I just threw up in the bathroom. Do you want everyone to get sick?"

"Wait here."

She walks over to knock on the captain's door.

"Yes?" the captain answers, opening the door to the cockpit.

"Captain, we have an ill passenger who wishes to exit the plane."

"Where are they?"

"It's the gentleman right over there, next to the hatch."

They both walk over to John and look at him suspiciously.

"Sir, are you okay to fly?"

"No, I'm nauseous and dizzy. I have to leave, *now!*" John shouts, hoping his crazy antics will get him out of the plane quicker.

"Okay, sir, please calm down. I will call the airline's medical team and have them escort you out."

The medical team arrives, and they escort John out of the plane and into the airline's clinic to give him a quick checkup.

"Sir, I don't find anything wrong with you. Your temperature is exactly 98.6, which is perfect. Your blood pressure is a bit high but that might just be your nerves," says the nurse. "Have you ever flown before?"

"No, maybe that's it. I might just be nervous. I'm sorry about all of this."

"Not a problem, sir. This happens more times than you'd think. I'll let the airlines know you're okay to fly."

"No need, I think I'll stay here a little while longer."

"Okay. Well then, you're free to go."

"Thank you so much. Again, I'm really sorry about all of this," John apologizes, and then storms out of the airport and hails a cab.

"Where to?"

"3351 Croydon Ave, as quickly as possible, please."

. . . .

John's cab pulls up to Sarah's place, and he jumps out before it can come to a full stop.

He runs up her steps, rings the bell and knocks as hard as he can.

No answer.

All of the lights are off. No one appears to be home, so he jumps back in the cab and heads over to the strip club, leaving the meter running.

He asks everyone and anyone if they've seen her, but no one has; she never returned to work.

Fearing the worst, he heads back over to her place, runs up the steps and kicks down the door.

"Sarah!" he shouts, not hearing a response, just the wood creaking beneath his feet.

He searches everywhere on the first floor for her, turning on the lights in each room, looking through every closet and open space, but there's still no sign of her.

"Sarah!" he shouts again, and this time he hears someone's muffled voice coming from upstairs.

"Sarah?"

The muffles increase.

He heads to the living room and finds a staircase to the second floor. Everything is pitch-black except for a small light shining through the edges of one door.

As he walks up the steps, he remembers the dream he once had when he saw Sarah and Lucas in bed together.

When he gets to the top, he takes a deep breath and slowly turns the doorknob, praying that his nightmare won't come true.

Sarah's muffles are now louder than ever as she watches the door slowly creak open.

He opens the door to find her naked, beaten, bloodied, gagged and tied up to her bed, and immediately rushes over to her.

Her eyes widen in fright as he removes the tape from her mouth. "Nooo!!" she screams.

Before John can turn around, Lucas cracks him over the head with the pistol grip of his gun and knocks him out cold, causing his body to slump over Sarah's.

Lucas unties her from the bed and points his pistol at John. "Drag your precious boyfriend's body downstairs to the basement, *now*."

Frantic that he would kill them both immediately if she refuses, she does as he says and moves John's heavy body down each step and into the basement.

Lucas sits John upright in the middle of the floor and cuffs his hands behind his back.

"Stand over there. If you move, I'll shoot you both, him first," he warns, pointing his gun at a rusty metal pole.

She walks over to it, holding her shivering naked body.

He then throws a bucket of water on John, and he slowly gains consciousness.

Lucas crouches in front of him, staring emotionlessly into his eyes. "You just couldn't leave her alone, could you? You had to try to save her. For what? To end up like this?"

John's eyes look past Lucas and directly at Sarah. "Love," he answers, showing no sign of fear even though he's petrified within.

"Oh, really? *Love*? Tell me. What's love, John?

John doesn't answer, refusing to play this game.

"I asked you a question. What's *love*, John!" Lucas shouts, grabbing his face and pointing the pistol into his mouth.

"No! No, no, no! Lucas, *please!*" Sarah screams.

He removes the gun from inside John's mouth and points it at her instead. "Do you have an answer?"

She keeps quiet.

"It's something you'll never know, never feel and never have," John responds, bringing Lucas' attention back to him.

"Well then, please explain. What is it that you love? Is it Sarah? Is it your family?" Lucas points the gun at Sarah's stomach. "How about your kid?"

John drops his head.

Confusion is written on Sarah's face. She's felt nauseous and vomited several times while strapped to the bed, but she thought it was her nerves from her body detoxing. In hindsight, it all makes sense: she and John didn't use protection the last time they were together.

"Answer me!" Lucas yells, walking over and pressing the barrel of his gun into Sarah's abdomen.

John keeps his head down and says a prayer underneath his breath, knowing the worst is about to occur.

Lucas laughs hysterically. "Oh, I see. Your love is for God, isn't it? Tell me, John, are you a man of faith?"

John picks up his head and stares fearlessly back at Lucas.

"Interesting"—Lucas smirks—"so where's your god right now? A man with your faith, surely he would come down with his white horse and save you, wouldn't he?"

John remains silent, but continues to stare him down.

Lucas puts his hand up to his ear as if he's trying to listen closely. "Hello? Is anyone there!" he shouts, looking around the room. "Nope. I don't hear anyone, do you? Wait, hold on...is that...is that *thee* Almighty!" Lucas mocks, laughing like a psychotic man off of his meds. "No! It's not. There's no one else here except for you, me and this whore. Don't you see, John? There is no god. It's all in your mind. It's all just false hope, just like Sarah. You see, you thought she was this *pure* woman, but it turns out that she's just another average-looking junky who's willing to spread her legs for her next high. If only—" Lucas chuckles "—if only you could have seen how she wrapped her pretty lips around the cocks of random men, or how she spread her legs like a gymnast in the back alley for a bump then *maybe* you would of left her alone."

John looks at Sarah, tortured by the thought.

"Life isn't a fairytale, John! What you fantasize about will *not* come true. It's false hope! It's *all* a lie! You should've left her alone while you had the chance, but you *insisted* and wouldn't go away. So now you're forced to choose. Let's see how strong your faith *really* is."

Lucas presses his gun on Sarah's temple, and she falls to her knees in a panic, screaming and pleading for her life.

"Shhh," Lucas hisses. "Let's see how much he *really* loves you, sweetheart."

John clinches his jaw in fright.

"You have two choices, John. Tell me you love her more than this imaginary god of yours, and I will let her live. Refuse, and she dies. It's that simple. What's it going to be? Your fictitious god or Sarah?"

They play chicken for a few seconds until Lucas grows impatient and pulls down the hammer of his gun, and the sound of the bullet loading into the gun's chamber trickles through the nerves beneath John's skin.

"It's okay, John," Sarah lets out, shaking from head to toe. She won't allow him to have to make this decision. If it's her time to go, she will do so knowing it was her choice.

John shakes his head.

"You have ten seconds to make your choice." Lucas points at an old-fashioned clock on the wall. "10 . . . 9 . . ."

John knows if he chooses God, Lucas will definitely kill her and the baby to prove a point. But if he chooses Sarah, evil will triumph. He's left to decide what is most important to him: his own destiny or God's will?

"4 . . . 3 . . ."

Sarah tries her best to contain her nerves.

"What's it going to be!" Lucas shouts, tapping on the trigger.

John shakes uncontrollably, sickened to his stomach, and gags from the thought of losing Sarah and Layla.

"2 . . ."

Time slows down and a calm falls over John as he realizes this is far greater than him. He holds firm, picks up his head, and stares back at Lucas with his chin held high and answers: "GOD."

Lucas slowly pushes down on the trigger, hoping John will plead for him to stop. But John remains still, not budging an inch or uttering a word—though he looks at Sarah with deep sorrow as flashes of his many lives with her and Layla flood his mind.

Lucas changes his plan as he realizes John will not succumb to the pressure: he removes the gun from Sarah's temple and points it at him instead. "Tell your god I said hello!" he shouts, shooting John between the brows of his eyes.

"Nooo!!" Sarah screams, running over to John, without any concern for her own life. She holds him in her arms as he sits lifeless in his own pull of blood. "Kill me," she

106

pleads, hoping Lucas would end it quickly so she wouldn't have to live another day without her love. *"Kill me!"*

Lucas kneels down, sticks his hands into John's blood on the ground, rubs it around his fingers, then places his hands on her face. "I hope you guys enjoy forever together," he torments, right before pointing his gun into his own mouth and shooting himself.

She doesn't blink an eye as she witnesses him take his own life. She's so full of hate, she only wishes she could've pulled the trigger herself.

Covered in their blood, she rocks back and forth with John in her arms. "I'm so sorry. I'm so, so sorry."

And as she caresses his face, she feels a faint breath on her hand. "John?" she cries, shaking him. "John!"

She lays him down, runs upstairs to the kitchen and calls 9-1-1.

13

CHAPTER THIRTEEN

THE POLICE AND PARAMEDICS RUSH IN and Sarah screams for help. She fumbles over her words and points toward the basement.

They immediately rush downstairs and find John and Lucas lying in a massive pool of blood.

"One has a pulse!" an EMT shouts, as they place John on a gurney to rush him to the hospital.

A police officer clothes Sarah with his jacket. "What's your name, honey?" he asks, but gets no answer. "What's your name?" he asks again.

She sits silent, dazed, and stares into space.

"She's in shock," says another EMT, who points a small flashlight in her eyes to show him her dilated pupils. "Let's get her clothed and take her in."

. . . .

The emergency doors fly open and doctors storm to John's aide while Sarah is placed in a separate room to be examined and questioned.

As half the staff of the trauma unit rush to save John's life, Sarah sits silently in her own little world as nurses, police investigators and a psychiatrist walk in and out of her hospital room.

"Sarah, I know this is hard for you but we need some answers."

She stares blankly into the officer's eyes.

"It's going to take some time for her to face reality. She's deeply traumatized," says the psych.

He ignores her.

"Sarah, can you tell me anything about John and Lucas' relationship?"

"John?" Sarah's eyes widen, breaking out of her shock. "John!!" she screams, tussling with the sheets to get out of bed.

"Sweetie, you have to lie down," says a nurse, trying her best to ease Sarah back into bed.

"Get off of me!" she screams, shoving the nurse to the side and trying to make her way out of the room.

The officers pin her back into bed, and the psychiatrist gives her a sedative.

Sarah's vision becomes blurred and her words slur, "John…Joh..Jo—"

. . . .

"Sarah, how are you feeling? Do you know where you are?"

She slowly opens her eyes, barely able to see who or what's in front of her; her body's heavy, mind is fogged, and it's hard to form words.

"My name is Dr. Emilia White, and I am your psychiatrist for the time you are here. You've been admitted to Loring Hall, a psychiatric facility, for evaluation."

Sarah tries to sit up, but can't.

"You're with child. We had to ensure his or her safety." Dr. White starts to remove the restraints on Sarah's hands and feet. "I am here to help you."

"Where's John?"

The look on Dr. White's face isn't promising. "He's fighting."

"I want to see him, I need to. I have to see him"—Sarah's eyes flood with tears—"*please.*"

Dr. White exhales, feeling her pain. "Like I said, I am here to help you. When I see that you're able to handle it, I promise you, I will *personally* take you to him. But my priority is your safety, above all. Do you understand?" Dr. White leans in close, placing her hand on Sarah's. "You've been through several traumatic experiences that are likely to cause severe post-traumatic stress. You've been raped, your body's currently going through withdrawal, and you're carrying a child, whose father is either fighting for his life or has already pas—"

"It's John's, no one else's but his."

"Okay, but regardless of whom the father is this child *needs* to be protected. And before I can allow you to leave, I need to be positive that both you and the baby are safe."

Sarah nods her head lightly, looks down at her stomach and smiles. "Okay. Whatever I have to do, I'll do it—but only if you promise to let me see him."

"You have my word."

"He has to meet her," Sarah weeps as she rubs her stomach.

"Meet who?"

"Her," she repeats, as she continues to caress her belly.

Dr. White looks at her as if she's deranged. "You're not even showing. You're at the earliest stage of pregnancy. How can you know it's a girl?"

"I just do," she answers, remembering John's story of Layla. "He'd always tell me he was made for me, and I for him, now look at what we've made together."

. . . .

Walking down the cold hallway of the intensive care unit, Sarah grips tight onto Dr. White's side as they get closer to John's room.

"Remember what we spoke about, Sarah. This is going to be hard at first, but you have to try to stay strong."

Sarah nods, taking deep breaths.

Standing in front of John's window, Dr. White signals the nurses to open the blinds.

Sarah's world slows down, her knees buckle and the air is immediately taken from her. "John!" she wails; nothing could've ever prepared her to see him in this way.

Dr. White keeps her from falling and holds her tight, and the nurses quickly close the blinds.

"No! No, please!" she cries out, tapping on the window.

"Are you sure?" Dr. White asks.

"Yes, I'm sure. I want to go in, I *need* to. He needs me."

Dr. White looks at the nurses, and they nod in agreement.

"You can sit over here," says one nurse, placing a seat by John's bedside.

Sarah walks slowly into the room. "Can I?"

"Yes, you can hold his hand."

Sarah's hand shakes uncontrollably as she reaches for his. And when her fingers touch his palm, all goes silent—not a sound in the world is heard except for the beating of his pulse, and no sound was ever more beautiful.

As Sarah sits beside him and lays her head on his palm, Dr. White and the nurses leave the room.

An hour and a half later, Dr. White walks back into John's room.

"Sarah, I have to take you back to your room now."

"But I don't want to go. I want to stay here with him."

"I'm sorry, Sarah, but you can't stay with him."

"Well, that's not necessarily true," one nurse intervenes. "Critically ill patients are allowed to have at least one person stay with them overnight."

Sarah gasps with joy. "So I can stay!"

"But that doesn't apply to those who are patients themselves," Dr. White counters. "Remember, Sarah, you are a patient—my patient."

"*Please*, Dr. White."

"No, Sarah. You've had your time. I have to look out for your well-being. We went over this."

The nurse steps in front of Dr. White. "This man is hanging on by a thread. He needs love and support around him, and she gives him that. He can go any day. This could be her only time left with him. Do you really want to be the one to take that away?"

Dr. White looks over at Sarah, whose eyes stare back in desperation. "If I release you, will you keep a promise?"

"Yes, of course."

"You have to promise to check in with me every day."

"Don't worry, I won't be going anywhere. I'm going to be right here with him. But yes, of course, I'll check in every day."

"Okay, then I'll go get your release forms."

Day and night, as Sarah vowed, she remains by John's side. But not a moment goes by that she doesn't wrestle with her conscience, not only for the guilt she feels for the lifestyle she has led—which she believes landed John in the position he is in—but also because she knows she must make the hardest phone call of her life.

Gabe wakes to the vibration of his phone and is confused by the 310 number. "Hello?"

"John..." she lets out, unable to pull the right words from out of her mouth.

"Sorry, this isn't John. This is his brother. You have the wrong number."

She starts to hyperventilate, and Gabe can hear the terror in her voice.

"Hey, calm down. Are you okay?"

"J--J-John," she stammers.

Her voice sounds so familiar to him by the way John's name rolls off of her tongue. "Sarah? Sarah, is that you?"

"J--J-John," she tries again, but her tongue is glued to her throat.

"Is everything okay?"

"John's hurt, Gabe. He's hurt. You have to get here," she finally lets out, squeezing out every bit of courage she has.

Gabe's heart drops. "What do you mean he's hurt?"

Anxiety overwhelms Sarah and panic sets in. She begins to stammer again. "H--h-he's...he's shot."

"Shot? What do you mean he's shot! Where is he?"

The pressure becomes too much and Sarah collapses, dropping the phone on the ground.

"Where is he!" Gabe continues to shout.

The nurses rush over to Sarah's aid.

"Hello? Hello! Answer me! Is anyone there? Hello!"

A nurse picks up the phone and explains everything that has happened—as well as John's state of health—and gives him all the information he needs to get to the hospital.

· · · · · · · · · · · · · · · · · · · ·

JOHN'S FAMILY STORM INTO THE HOSPITAL and is directed straight to his room. His mother screams and breaks down at the sight of her boy lying virtually dead, on life support.

"Get off of my brother," Gabe threatens Sarah, holding her responsible for John's condition.

She jumps, startled by the tone of his voice, and immediately lets go of John's hand. "I'm sorry," she weeps, quickly getting up and walking past Gabe and his family. But although she leaves John's room, she does not leave the hospital. She's determined to stay and support John, even if that means she has to wait for her time by sitting on the floor outside of his room and endure the gut-wrenching screams of his mother.

Dr. Bachmann, the hospital surgeon, enters John's room to address the family.

"Tell me my baby will be okay, *please*, Doctor!" Gail shouts, frantically grabbing on his coat and falling to her knees. "Tell me he's going to be okay!"

Dr. Bachmann doesn't look like he's come with good news. "Mrs. Harper, we're doing all that we can for your son."

Jim picks up his wife and holds her in his arms. "Please, tell us our boy is going to be okay."

"If you may"—Dr. Bachmann gestures to the empty chairs in the room—"please take a seat."

Jim, Gail and Gabe sit down, holding each other tightly and bracing themselves for bad news.

"As you are aware, John has suffered a gunshot wound to the head. The bullet has ruptured the frontal bone of his cranium but, fortunately, stopped just short of the cerebral cortex. However, we did have to extract several fragments of his shattered skull from his brain, so it is too early to assess the damage that has been done to his frontal lobe. For now, he is day to day. It's a miracle he's even alive."

"What are his chances?" Gabe asks.

Dr. Bachmann takes a moment, trying to figure out the easiest way to break it to them. "I'd give it a 30% chance he'll come out of this coma. If he doesn't show any signs of recovery soon, it'll be a few months to a year until his body completely shuts down."

Gail tries to keep her composure, rocking silently in her seat and tugging on Jim's jacket as he sits breathless, and Gabe storms out of the hospital.

Pacing back and forth, blocks from the hospital, Gabe grieves the only way he knows how, through anger. "Why would you leave your family for a girl!" he shouts at the top of his lungs, looking up at the sky as if he were talking to John himself. "How could you? How could you leave me without a brother?" he weeps, leaving no emotion suppressed. "You better come back! You better, John! *Please*, please come back."

He stays outside for a while until he can gather himself, but soon makes his way back inside to take his father's place, allowing Jim to walk away and grieve on his own, away from all eyes.

. . . .

ONE MONTH, SEVEN DAYS, FOUR HOURS and thirty-two aching minutes later, nothing has changed: John shows no progress; Gail still weeps by his bedside; Jim tries his best to be strong; and Gabe's anger still burns red-hot.

Looking out from John's window, Gabe scowls at Sarah, who's sitting across the hall by herself with her face in her palms as she prays for John's recovery.

Jim makes his way over to Gabe. "Son—"

"Who is she to pray for anything? If it wasn't for her, this would've never happened. John was a fool to love such a person."

Jim remains silent, allowing his son to rant.

"If she wasn't such a whore, she would've stayed with my brother, and he wouldn't have had to chase. He wouldn't have gone to California, and he wouldn't have..." Gabe chokes up. "Am I right?"

Jim consoles his son and shakes his head lightly.

"No, no you're not, neither are your mother and I." He turns to look over at his wife, and she nods her head. "It isn't right to shun her like this."

"What are you talking about? Look at your son." Gabe points at John. "She did this!"

"No, she didn't. She left and John chased, because he loved her. He loved her more than anything—more than me, more than your mother and more than you. Whether we want to believe it or not, it is the truth."

Gabe's eyes redden.

"When you love someone, Gabe, you're bound to love who they love—and damn it I love my boy. So if he loves her, then I love her—and you should too."

Gabe shakes his head as tears fly off his face. "I can't. I won't."

"You can. You need to for John."

Gabe breaks down on his father's shoulder.

"Go on, Gabe. Show her love. It's what your brother would want. Show her the love that he can't."

Gail lays John's hand down and walks over to them, taps Gabe on the shoulder and hugs him tight. "Go do what's right, my boy. Honor your brother."

Gabe takes a step back, stands in silence, and absorbs what they've had to say. He thinks about John and all of the times he's seen him genuinely happy, and all of those times were always shared with Sarah.

Without another moment to think, he makes his way over to her.

As a shadow falls over Sarah, she looks up and sees Gabe. Her sorrowful eyes stare up at him and her mouth quivers.

He looks back, takes a seat next to her and simply holds her tight, and she breaks down in his arms. No words are shared between the two, just love.

"You've done good," says Gail, as she rests her head on Jim's shoulder.

He exhales. "It's not enough."

She looks up at him, confused.

"You have to make the call."

She understands, nods, and walks away.

The hands of the clock seem to tick slower with every breath during that call. But thirty minutes later, it is done.

"She's on her way," Gail tells Jim, placing her cell into her pocket and walking back over to him.

He smiles, brings her into his arms and kisses her on her forehead. "John would be so proud."

Gail looks up at him and shakes her head. "Not yet, we still have one more thing to do."

He understands her clearly, and they make their way over to Sarah, embracing her with all the love they have to give.

. . . .

"Good morning, everyone. John has another visitor. We're going to have to ask one person to leave. There can't be more than four people in this room at a time," says Amy, one of the nurses.

"We'll go," Jim and Gail answer. "Gabe, you too. Come on."

"Huh? Why?"

"Just come on, Gabe," Jim commands.

"No, you guys stay. You're his family. I'll go."

"No, Sarah, please stay," Gail insists.

All three leave the room and in comes Lynn: Sarah's mother.

Frozen in place, Sarah can't believe her eyes.

Lynn doesn't utter a word. She's too choked up and can't possibly express how much she's missed her little girl—or how glad she is to see her alive—and Sarah can't find the right words to apologize for all the wrongs she's done. But all the anger and resentment between the two fades as Sarah simply walks into her mother's arms, shedding tears.

14
CHAPTER FOURTEEN

EIGHT MONTHS HAVE PASSED, and Sarah still remains by John's bedside, even though she can go into labor any day. Every day she takes it upon herself to bathe him and help his caretakers in any way that she can. She only hopes that her love will bring him back the same way his love has done for her, because although she has never fought for her life in the way he is now, his unconditional love for her pieced hers back together. When she had no hope, no love and no way out, he was her hope, her love, and her light out of the darkness. And at a price, he now lies in his own abyss as he dreams a never-ending dream in his comatose state.

John's in the same position as when he got shot: faced down, eyes shut, hands cuffed behind his back and sitting in his own pool of blood. It's as if time has stopped and nothing has progressed. The only change is that he's no longer in Lucas' basement, but back in the dreadful forest where he had his first dream.

"Wake up!! Wake up, John!" Satan yells, still disguised in John's image.

John slowly lifts his head, trembling in pain, opens his eyes and tries to peek through the blood that's pouring down his face.

Satan laughs. "I told you, John. *This* is reality. It's just you here sitting alone. I didn't do this to you. You did this to yourself. Those handcuffs? They don't exist. They are only symbolic to the prison that you set yourself in. You're trapped in this fantasy world where you believe that a higher being controls life when, in reality, *you* control it. You can set yourself free if only you stop believing in this false god and love for a girl you're not meant to be with. I tried to warn you that this world inside your head didn't exist, but you chose to believe differently. What good did that do you?"

John doesn't utter a word. He only stares desperately into the distance where he first saw his family from heaven, but the darkness that enveloped them does not give in.

"Answer me, John."

He gets no response.

Angered and impatient, Satan screams in John's face, "Answer me!"

Still, John remains silent.

Satan laughs like a madman. "What can you possibly be thinking about? Do you think if you stay silent for long enough all of this will go away? Do you *think* if you ignore me you'll somehow wake up from this?" Satan kneels down to look into John's eyes. "No! You won't! Not until you realize your thoughts are nothing more than a fantasy. Until then, this is where you'll remain for *eternity*—along with this pain!" he shouts, placing his fingers into John's head wound.

John bites down on his tongue, refusing to give Satan the satisfaction of hearing him scream.

"This pain that you feel in your head is nothing more than your mind trying to free itself from these crazed, psychotic thoughts. It's tired of your fantasies, John! It wants to be freed, so *release it!*"

"No," John weeps.

"Why? What has this fantasy of yours done for you? What has this god of yours done, other than cause you pain? *Look at yourself.* You've done good unto others, followed all the rules that you possibly could, yet you're still here. Where has this fantasy led you? *Nowhere.* But I'll tell you this, it has done something. It's driven you mad, caused you to imagine a life that you could never have. You're trapping yourself into your own misery. Become your own god and rise up out of it!"

John tries his best to ignore him and whispers a prayer, over and over again.

"Shut up," Satan demands. "That won't help you."

John ignores him and continues.

"I said, shut—"

*　　　*　　　*　　　*　　　*
　　*　　*　　　　*　　*
*　　　*　　　*　　　*　　　*

The heavens are silent as the Angels watch down on John's tortured soul, knowing there is nothing they can do to help, until {{THUNDER SOUNDS}} and out comes a blinding light that even they can't see past.

The light shines upon Layla, and God's voice speaks out:

"MY CHILD, IT IS TIME."

*   *   *   *   *
    *   *   *   *
*   *   *   *   *

"—shut up!" Satan screams, pacing back and forth, as John continues to pray:

"LORD, I am not worthy to receive you, but only say the word and my soul shall be healed."

And with those words, comes a white light flickering in the distance that increases as John's faith strengthens. The light then begins to tear through the darkness like a river breaking through a dam.

"Be quie—" Satan tries to speak, but is muted. He's then brought to his knees and forced to sit face to face with the product of God.

John stares deep into Satan's eyes as his wounds begin to heal, clothes become white and hands are freed from their restraints. He then leans toward Satan and whispers three subtle, beautiful words: "GOD is LOVE."

The light then swallows up the abyss and leaves no darkness behind, not a shade or shadow.

The sky regains its color; the trees blow in the wind, rivers rush and animals roam—but not a sound is heard. All is quiet until the silence is broken by the laughter of a young girl.

Out from the light, running up a hill, comes a 4-year-old girl with a smile as big as Sarah's.

Layla runs with her hands spread out, brushing through the tall palm grass, and John slowly walks toward her, quickly falling to his knees in awe of how beautiful she is. She jumps into his arms, and he holds her tight.

"Let's go get Mommy," Layla whispers into his ear, pulling back from her hug to look into his eyes. She then wraps her tiny hand around his left ring finger to help him get back onto his feet, and they walk into the light, together.

Sarah's water breaks, and her contractions get stronger and closer together. She's quickly rushed into a delivery room.

"No, I can't do this!" she cries out.

Her mother tries to console her. "Shhh, everything is going to be all right."

"I can't."

"Yes you can, Sarah. We're here with you," says Gail, as she rubs her hand.

"But he should be here," Sarah weeps.

Gail looks away, trying to contain her emotions. "He is. He's always with you."

The door opens and in comes the nurses. They begin to set up equipment beside Sarah's bed.

"What is all of this?" Sarah nervously asks.

Rosa, a nurse, turns to her. "He may not be conscious, but he'll be here with you, through it all."

Those words ring in Sarah's mind, causing her to have a vision of John speaking to her just before their rebirth: "I love you, sweetheart. We shall rise out of love, through all."

They then roll John in, and tears flood down Sarah's face.

. . . .

Lynn coaches Sarah through delivery, trying to sooth her by placing a damp cloth on her forehead. "Good job, baby, *breathe*."

Sarah grabs and squeezes John's hand tight each time she pushes. "I need you!" she cries out to him. "*We* need you."

She pushes, and pushes, and pushes.

"Here comes the head!" the doctor shouts. "Keep pushing, Sarah. We're almost done. You're doing great!"

"John!!" she screams out for him one last time, pushing out their child.

Gail and Lynn grow quiet, biting at their nails, as they watch their grandchild being delivered.

"It's a girl!" the doctor shouts.

And as GOD breathes the breath of life into the lungs of Layla...he does the same for John, allowing his eyes to open to the sweet sound of her beautiful cry.

Author's note:

It is not my intention to confuse or manipulate the reader into believing in this story's interpretation of the biblical verses. I chose to use the verses in an unorthodox manner in order to drive the story forward and to express what I feel are some of the *many* purposes the holy book serves: to shine truth on faith, love and forgiveness—above which there are no greater laws.

CPSIA information can be obtained at www.ICGtesting.com
Printed in the USA
BVOW08s0318070916

461356BV00003B/9/P